ROOTED IN MURDER

MAPLE SYRUP MYSTERIES

EMILY JAMES

STRONGHOLD BOOKS

Editor: Christopher Saylor at www.saylorediting.wordpress.com/services/

Cover Design: Deranged Doctor Design at www.derangeddoctordesign.com

Published April 2019 by Stronghold Books

Ebook ISBN: 978-1-988480-37-4; Print ISBN: 978-1-988480-38-1; Large Print ISBN: 978-1-988480-43-5

ALSO BY EMILY JAMES

Maple Syrup Mysteries

Sapped: A Maple Syrup Mysteries Prequel

A Sticky Inheritance

Bushwhacked

Almost Sleighed

Murder on Tap

Deadly Arms

Capital Obsession

Tapped Out

Bucket List

End of the Line

Slay Bells Ringing

(also contains a Cupcake Truck Mystery novella)

Rooted in Murder

Guilty or Knot

Stumped

Cupcake Truck Mysteries

Sugar and Vice

A Sampling of Murder (Coming Soon!)

For my husband. Because the person who shares the best and worst parts of your life really deserves two books dedicated to them.

If you tell the truth, you don't have to remember anything.

— MARK TWAIN

1
_____

"*H*e's saying the land isn't ours." The whistle of wind in the background made it difficult to hear Russ' voice through the truck's speakers. "So we can't plant the trees."

I pulled over and parked Mark's truck. We'd swapped vehicles this morning because it was easier for me to take Velma to the vet in his truck. Unfortunately, I wasn't as comfortable driving it while talking as I was my car. "What do you mean the land isn't ours?"

I'd spent the last few weeks, since Mark and I returned from our abbreviated honeymoon, negotiating a deal for us to buy the farmland next to Sugarwood. We wanted to expand the size of our sugar bush.

The deal should have been finalized last week.

"He didn't get the paperwork to sign," Russ said.

I grimaced. I should have followed up when I hadn't heard from our lawyer that everything was done. I'd assumed that no news was good news, and I'd been busy working at my own law firm.

My partner, Anderson, had taken on a couple of pro bono cases involving minors—I suspected as an attempt to impress the public defender he was currently dating—and I'd gotten roped into helping build their cases. Even though they were both guilty, both also seemed remorseful. We were trying to work plea deals to get them probation and community service rather than having them end up in juvenile detention.

It wasn't the same as defending people who were innocent, which was what I preferred, but it still felt good trying to help minors pay their debt to society without ruining their future.

My busy days weren't an excuse, though. I still had responsibilities as part-owner of Sugarwood. "I'll go by McClanahan and Associates and figure out what happened."

Russ's breathing gained a bit of a wheeze like he was working while talking to me. "Make sure he knows we need this figured out fast. These saplings are gonna die if we don't plant them soon."

We also had such a small seasonal window to plant them. Russ said there was debate over whether it was better to plant new sugar maples in the fall or in the winter. The man he'd learned the business from in his younger days swore by planting them in the winter, shortly before the weather turned, so that's what we'd decided to do. Unfortunately, it meant we were playing a game of weather roulette in order to plant the new trees this year. We needed to get it done before the sap started to run. That happened at a different time every year, depending on the weather.

"I'll take care of it," I said.

Static answered me, and the call dropped. Russ must have walked through one of Fair Haven's infamous cellphone black holes.

Velma whined softly behind me, and I stuck my fingers back through the grate that turned the truck's back seat into a giant crate. "Just a small detour, I promise."

She'd gotten a nail in her paw while Mark and I were away, and the vet had finally cleared her today to run around again. I'd promised her a long walk in the woods before dark. While I knew she didn't actually understand English, I'd still made a promise. Besides, if I didn't let her burn off some of her energy, Mark and I would have another long evening trying to keep her out of trouble in the house.

I parked in front of McClanahan & Associates, climbed out, and then used the remote start button to turn the truck on again to keep Velma warm.

It wasn't until I stepped inside that I realized I'd been hoping Ashley Jenkins was out sick with the stomach bug currently going around.

She wasn't. She perched behind the desk in the reception area, a tight black V-neck sweater exposing almost a third of her cleavage. It'd probably been a long-shot hope anyway that she'd be out sick. Based on the fact that her nose was smaller and straighter than the last time I'd seen her, I'd place a bet that she used all her sick days and vacation days on a nose job.

She tilted her chin down and leveled a cold stare at me over the top of her glasses. They were new, too. "You don't have an appointment."

Not for the first time I felt like snarkily asking *What did I ever do to you?* Except I knew the answer. I married Mark Cavanaugh. According to the Fair Haven rumor mill, Ashley had been angling to get him to ask her out ever since his first wife died. Mark hadn't dated anyone at all until I came along.

I pasted on my jury-ready smile—confident but not cocky. I hoped that was how it looked anyway. I'd been practicing it. "I'm here following up on the paperwork for a property purchase. The seller says his lawyer never received it from you."

Her lips pushed out like she'd intended to purse them, but they were too full of dermal filler for it to work. "He's clearly mistaken. I sent them myself the same day you signed them. I can't be held responsible if his lawyer is disorganized and irresponsible."

There was an edge to the way she looked at me, almost like she was daring me to contradict her. She'd once failed to enter an appointment I'd booked with Tom McClanahan into their system, but this was taking things too far. This was interfering with my business.

And I had absolutely no proof.

I shrugged as if I had all the time in the world to deal with the missing paperwork. "Things happen. I'm headed that direction right now anyway for another appointment. I can drop off replacement copies."

Ashley made a consoling *mmm* sound. "I'm really sorry, but gathering up the paperwork will take some time. I'm swamped with other work, and I wouldn't be able to get it ready in time. You'd be late for your other appointment. But I'll get it out this week."

She'd trapped me into a game of *you know that I know that you know*. We both knew I didn't have another appointment. And we both knew that, if I left, those papers might not make it there this week.

All I could think as we stood there looking at each other was that I was tired of sparring with her. Maybe it was that I hadn't been feeling well this morning or that hours of work and a forest's worth of baby trees were at stake. Whatever the case, if Ashley kept this up, I was going to need to switch to another lawyer. It'd be a sad day for me since Tom McClanahan had been my Uncle Stan's lawyer. I trusted him.

I couldn't hold back a sigh. "Is Tom in?"

Ashley sniffed and turned her gaze to her computer screen, a clear brush-off. "He's with a client, and you don't have an appointment. If you'd like to speak to him, his first opening is next Monday afternoon."

No more playing this game with her. No more talking. She was getting on my nerves more today than she usually did, and the last thing I wanted to do was say something I'd regret later.

I checked that Mark's truck was still running and dropped down into a chair where I could watch the truck while also being the first thing Tom saw when he came out of his office.

A throat clearing noise came from her direction. "The waiting area is only for clients with appointments."

What was she going to do? Physically remove me? She was taller, but I probably had ten pounds of muscle on her. Call the police? I was related to some of the officers by marriage and most of the others had been over to my house to dinner in the past year.

Instead of replying, I leaned back and crossed my arms. A few minutes later, I had to restart the truck again. The fact that leaving the truck running like that wasn't environmentally responsible made me want to snap at Ashley more.

The only thing that kept me calm and quiet was a little voice in my head that sounded an awful lot like Mark's mom whispering that the meanest people were the ones in the most pain. On one level, I knew she was right. On another level, it still felt like an easy way to excuse bad behavior.

The door to Tom's office opened, and a couple in their forties came out. They headed over to Ashley's desk, and I ducked into Tom's office while she was distracted.

The difference between Tom and Ashley never got old. She looked like she was spending all her money to compensate for something missing on the inside. He seemed comfortable with the fact that he had thinning hair and was the same height as the average woman. The last time I'd been in his office, he'd shown me a picture of his family. His wife was a good two inches taller than him. They hadn't even let the photographer pose them in such a way as to minimize the difference.

He glanced up from his papers and gave a little jerk like I wasn't the person he'd been expecting.

"Sorry to surprise you," I said, "but I have a major problem."

Tom moved around to the front of his desk. "Go ahead."

There was no hint of hurrying me in his voice even though I'd burst into his office. Still, Velma had now been trapped in Mark's truck for nearly half an hour. I quickly filled Tom in on the missing paperwork and my homeless trees.

He glanced at the door to his office like he might suspect

what had happened. "I'll take them over myself and hand them straight to Anthony, your seller's lawyer. We'll have this handled by the end of the business day today." His gaze slid to the door again. "I'm sorry for the mix-up."

Part of me wanted to ask him why he kept a receptionist who had the people skills of someone raised by wolves, but I swallowed it down. There was a time to rock the boat and a time to let it carry you calmly to shore. This felt like a *calmly to shore* kind of time.

I thanked him and hurried out to my truck. The couple was still booking their next appointment as I passed—thankfully.

I tried to call Russ as soon as I was back in the truck, but his cell phone went straight to voicemail, a sure sign he was still in a dead zone. I'd have to drive out there.

Hopefully Mr. Huffman was still there as well. If I explained to him that the papers would be at his lawyer's office by the end of the day, he might let us plant the trees anyway. It wasn't like it was any risk to him for us to do it. If the sale didn't go through, we'd be the ones who'd have to dig the trees back out again.

I drove past our driveway, and Velma whined from the backseat. She might not speak English, but she sure knew where home was.

Russ's truck, our tractor, and a few other employee vehicles I recognized were parked at the edge of the field. I pulled in next to them. Partway across the field, Russ and Mr. Huffman stood with squared shoulders, separate from the others. Mr. Huffman was talking with his hands. Loudly.

That didn't look good.

I let Velma out of the truck. The ground was still frozen

enough that I could put her back in after without coating Mark's truck in mud—he was fussy about that—and she could still burn off some energy.

Her feet barely hit the ground before she took off for the edge of the trees. She reminded me of a deer bounding across the field. Unlike how she tended to make a break for it when my friend Mandy took her for a walk, I knew she wouldn't go far enough away to lose sight of me. I'd worked hard on teaching her to stay within eyesight.

I strode across the field, trying to simultaneously look collected and not trip. The plowed ground meant I had to pick my way across mountains and crevasses. How Velma ran across this uneven terrain was beyond me.

I was ten feet away when Mr. Huffman turned in my direction. His face was red, and he bobbed on his feet in a way that reminded me of a tea kettle ready to boil over. Before we started dealing with Mr. Huffman, Russ described him as having a long fuse, but watch out when it finally blew.

Mr. Huffman pointed a finger at me. "I could have sold this place for ten percent more. I only made the deal with you because your uncle was a good neighbor who always helped out a friend in need. But if I don't have those papers soon—"

I held up a hand, palm toward him. "I personally went to our lawyer, and he assured me the papers would be there for you to sign by the end of the day."

Velma had moved away from the edge of the bush. She had her head down into one of the holes we'd dug for the new trees. Frozen dirt shot five feet out behind her. So much for her being relatively clean when I put her back in Mark's truck. I might have to walk her home and then catch a ride back to get the vehicle.

Mr. Huffman's head swiveled in her direction. "And now that monster dog of yours is adding to this gopher field. If you don't come good on this deal, it'll be on you to fill in all these holes."

Russ clapped a hand on Mr. Huffman's shoulder, something I never would have dared to do. "When have you ever known me to not come good on a promise, Wayne?"

I edged away and called for Velma. Her head popped up, then dropped down into the hole. She backed up, pulling a long, straight item with her. All that work just for a branch when she could have gotten one from the bush without all the effort of digging it up. Though maybe the digging was part of what made it fun for her.

I called her name again. She headed in our direction, dragging her treasure by one end. Silly dog. She had to know I wasn't going to let her chew it even if she managed to haul it all the way back to me. When she'd been teething, we'd already had to make a trip to the vet to have splinters removed from her mouth because she'd gnawed on a branch and I hadn't caught her in time. We didn't need a repeat of that. She'd just recovered from one injury.

I picked my way across the field toward her. Her find was awfully straight for a branch. And thicker at the end, like a bone.

I looked back over my shoulder. "Russ?" He and Mr. Huffman both turned in my direction. "Can she catch anything from an old animal bone? I think she dug one up."

I expected Mr. Huffman to stay behind or look annoyed, but

he trailed after Russ toward me.

Russ's trademark waddle actually looked more graceful than the way I'd stumbled across the field furrows. "Depends on what kind of animal and how old the bone is."

Mr. Huffman kept up to Russ as if the ground were flat. "Let me see it. I used to hunt before the arthritis made my hands ache."

Velma skirted around the men and came close enough that I could see her find but stayed far enough away that I couldn't take it from her. Whatever animal she dug up had to be a big one. Up close, I could now see that the smooth bone had knobby ends on both sides, as if one should attach to a hip socket and the other to a knee cap. Shouldn't a large animal like a deer or a cow be shaped differently? The horses we kept at Sugarwood didn't have bones anything like this one.

I got that fluttery feeling at the bottom of my throat, rising up my neck like my insides were scrabbling for means of escape. Neither of the men had said anything. "Is that a—"

"It's not like any animal bone I've ever seen," Mr. Huffman said.

"Me neither." Russ's voice had an almost accusatory quality to it.

Even though I knew he didn't actually blame me for all the murders that had happened in Fair Haven since I'd arrived, he did think I attracted death like a black car attracted dust.

There was only one thing I could think to do. I pulled out my phone, snapped a picture, and texted it to Mark. As county medical examiner, he'd seen more human bones than any of us. He'd resolve this one way or the other.

Velma dropped to the frozen ground, her hind end in the air and one paw holding down the bone while she gnawed on the end.

"Should we take it away from her?" Mr. Huffman asked. "Just in case."

I didn't want to touch it if it were a human bone, but Mr. Huffman had crossed his arms over his chest and Russ backed away a step. They clearly thought I should be the one. She was my dog, after all.

Human or animal, I didn't want to take the drool-covered bone from Velma's mouth with the cute, fuzzy white mittens my mother-in-law gave me for Christmas. I tugged them off my hands and held them out to Ross. "Trade me at least."

He snagged my mittens from me and practically threw his gloves in my direction. I edged toward Velma. Chances were she wouldn't want to relinquish her hold.

I scooped up a clump of dirt about the size of a tennis ball and made sure she saw it. I heaved the dirt ball off behind her. She didn't chase it, but she did drop her hold on the bone. I lunged in and grabbed it from her.

My cell phone vibrated in my pocket.

Bone in one hand, I wriggled off the other glove and fished out my phone.

Mark's picture flashed on my screen. "I don't know whether to hope that picture was a bad joke or not. Where are you? I'm in the car, and I need to know where to head."

The fluttering in my throat stopped and dropped like lead pellets into my stomach. "What kind of bone is it?"

"A human femur."

2

*O*fficer Quincey Dornbush arrived at the field only a few minutes after Mark and took our statements. By the time he finished, crime scene techs swarmed the field. Ross, Mr. Huffman, the Sugarwood employees who'd come to help plant the trees, and I were all evicted from the scene.

Part of me had hoped it was an isolated bone. That it was a hiker who died miles away, and a coyote dragged the bone here. I hoped it right up to the point when Mark texted to tell me they'd found a complete skeleton.

Apparently, it wouldn't matter if Tom McClanahan got those papers signed. No one would be planting anything until the police released the field.

I took Velma home, but my hands twitched, wanting to turn around. I wasn't used to being out of the loop when it came to dead bodies in Fair Haven. That skeleton could belong to someone I knew.

I waited up for Mark until he got home, even though I had

an early appointment tomorrow to go over some case files with Anderson. I even made spaghetti and meatballs and had a plate waiting for him. I'd never be a gourmet cook, but I was getting pretty decent at dishes that involved pasta.

Mark sank into his chair, his cheeks still pink from the cold. Early February in Michigan was a terrible time to have to do anything outside.

I sat on my hands to keep from fidgeting while he ate. So many of the people in this town were important to me. I had a suspicion I wouldn't be able to sleep until I knew they were all safe.

"Do you know anything yet?" I finally asked.

There was only so much Mark was allowed to tell me about his work due to confidentiality. I couldn't ask him too much directly. Part of what made us work as a couple was that I was comfortable with that part of his job. Until I'd joined my parents' law firm, I'd known very few details of the cases they worked, and my Uncle Stan's original career as a cardiologist meant he didn't talk specifics about work, either.

Mark reached a hand out towards me. "The bones were old."

I slid one of my hands into his. He either knew me exceptionally well—knowing what I was really worried about—or it was simply one of the only things he could actually share.

"How old?" I asked.

"Old enough that whatever happened took place when neither of us were in Fair Haven."

I did move to Fair Haven only a little over a year ago. Mark grew up here, and then moved away for school and work. He only returned after he and his first wife lost their unborn daughter. Saying neither of us was here when it happened still left a big window of time.

At least it meant I hadn't known the victim. They'd probably left behind people who loved them and would mourn them. Maybe it was selfish of me to be glad I wasn't that person this time. But I was glad.

I also couldn't be accused of having anything to do with the death. Chief McTavish and I had moved past the point where he thought I was killing people in order to solve their murders, but he'd also recently accused me of being some sort of psycho because I ended up investigating a missing person while Mark and I were on our honeymoon.

I'd just as soon steer clear of any involvement in this case even if it did leave me with no way to satisfy my curiosity. "Do they know who it is—was?"

"We were able to get a DNA match. He was in the system for some petty crimes. Quincey and McTavish are on their way to notify his next of kin now. Quincey said that, until tonight, everyone thought he'd just run off."

Mark brought his plate and glass together as if he meant to clean them up. I took them from him instead. Not only had he had a busier day than I had, but he'd been shouldering a lot of the work around the house while I'd been under the weather the last few days. I rinsed the dishes and slid them into the dishwasher. I wanted to know more, but there didn't seem to be much else I could ask that Mark would be able to answer.

Arms slid around my waist, and Mark trailed kisses up my neck. "How about we do something other than talk about death right now?"

This day had gotten off to a rough start, but at least it could end well. I turned around in Mark's hold and leaned into his kiss.

A knock rattled the front door.

Mark groaned and tilted his forehead against mine. "What are the chances this late at night that can be anything good?"

The newlywed part of me wanted to ignore the knock at the door and go back to what we'd been doing. The responsible part of me knew we couldn't. Even though I couldn't think of a reason someone would show up late at night rather than calling, that didn't mean there wasn't one. And Mark was right. Whoever it was wouldn't be here now unless it was important.

Another knock at the door, more insistent this time. A sleepy bark rolled out from the laundry room where the dogs were tucked into their crates for the night. Big dogs were a bit like babies. Once you put them down for the night, you didn't want to wake them. You'd have a hard time getting them back to sleep if you did.

Mark snatched another quick kiss. "Hold my place. I'll be right back."

I trailed Mark halfway to the door, so I could see who was there. Grady Sherwin stood on our doorstep, still in his Fair Haven police uniform. As if a late-night visitor wasn't bad enough, it had to be him.

Mark kept one hand on the door and pressed the other into the door frame, creating a human barrier. He probably didn't even know he was doing it. "Is there something that couldn't wait for morning?"

A tiny note of exhaustion tinged Mark's otherwise professional tone. As much as he loved his job, getting pulled back out into the winter night after a long day would test anyone's stamina.

"I'm not here for you." Grady looked around Mark, and his gaze landed on me. "I'm here for her."

Grady Sherwin and I had a rocky enough history that I wouldn't put it past him to come here with some routine question that could wait until morning just to reassert his authority. Despite how he'd helped clear Mark's name before Christmas, we weren't exactly friends.

I joined Mark at the door. "It's close to midnight, and I already gave my statement to Quincey. If you have other questions, I'd be happy to come in tomorrow afternoon, when I'm done at work."

Something flickered across Grady's face, fast enough I couldn't be sure it wasn't just the light casting shadows.

He placed a foot onto the door step. "I'm not here about the case. Not officially. I'm here to call in the favor you owe me."

In the back of my mind, I think I always believed that Grady Sherwin would never call in the favor I owed him. I'd made the deal back when Mark was accused of murder. We needed some old case files to prove him innocent, and Grady turned out to be the only one who could get them for us. Now, I felt like I was trapped in the old TV show *Once Upon a Time*, and Rumpelstiltskin had come to collect.

I'd keep my word, but I still had to question Grady's timing. Unless someone was dying—in which case he needed a doctor, not me—it was rude to show up at someone's house in the middle of the night. "And the favor couldn't have waited until morning?" I asked.

"No." Grady lightly shoved the door, and Mark stepped back out of his way.

The next thing I knew, Grady Sherwin stood in my living room—a place I'd never expected to see him.

Which meant I needed to accept the inevitable. The sooner I heard his favor, the sooner he'd get out of here.

I held my hand out in the direction of the kitchen table. "Then you might as well sit."

I could almost hear my mom lecturing me about rudeness across all the miles. The one thing that gave me solace was that she'd also lecture Grady for showing up like this in the first place.

Grady sat telephone pole-straight in the chair and crossed his heavily muscled arms. Not for the first time, I was struck by the fact that he must do a lot more weightlifting than cardio in the gym to have so many muscles and yet still have a belly that made him look six months pregnant.

"The skeleton you found belonged to Lee Mills," Grady said.

He had to be joking. He shouldn't be telling me anything like that.

Mark's mouth drooped open, then snapped shut.

Grady was telling the truth about the name. Was the favor that I not report him for breaching confidentiality?

"Okay..." I stretched the word out. My stomach had started to feel hard and tight, like the lining had magically transformed into old leather. "Where does the favor come in?"

If Grady had murdered this Lee Mills, I wasn't taking the fall for him. When I'd agreed to the favor, I'd also told him whatever it was had to be legal. Which, in hindsight, wasn't actually fair. He had done something borderline illegal for me. But still.

Besides, no one would believe I'd done it. I had no connections to Fair Haven that long ago.

The look Grady gave me said *Are you stupid or something?* "They're going to accuse my sister of killing him, and she'll need a lawyer."

Hadn't seen that one coming. Normally this was where I gave a spiel about how I only defended innocent people. I couldn't do that this time. Like it or not, I owed Grady. Regardless, I'd need to know.

"Did she do it?" I asked.

Grady's stare hardened into a glare. "That shouldn't matter for our deal."

Most people I liked more the longer I knew them. That definitely couldn't be said about Grady. "It doesn't. But you defend an innocent person differently than you do a guilty one."

Some of the cold iron left his expression. "You'll have to ask her, then."

The look on Mark's face said we shouldn't have opened the door. He got to his feet. "If this is about the case, I can't be here. Conflict of interest."

I wanted to shoot Mark a look that said *traitor* since he technically owed Grady for the favor he'd done as much as I did, but Mark was right. He couldn't be here.

"I need to head to bed anyway," Mark said.

And just like that, I went from anticipating one of the perks of married life to having to stay up late with one of my least favorite people in Fair Haven. The only person I liked less was Ashley from Tom McClanahan's office.

My mom's voice, though, was back in my head, admonishing me to offer him a cup of coffee. Unfortunately, Mark's mom would probably agree with her on that one.

I stood. "Can I get you something to drink?"

"I'd take a beer."

I was going to assume that meant he was scared for his sister and didn't know how to admit it. But I couldn't accommodate him. "Anything nonalcoholic?"

Grady raised both eyebrows as if to say *Really?* Like he thought I was criticizing him even though I wasn't.

"Coffee'll just keep me awake," he said.

I thought staying awake was the idea. If this took much longer, I was going to need some coffee. And tomorrow I'd need it pumped into my veins through an IV to stay awake.

At least neither of the mothers could say I hadn't tried to be hospitable.

I sank back into my seat. "Why don't you tell me why you think the police will suspect your sister?"

3

_G_rady pushed away from my table, scrapping his chair across the floor. "I'll take you to her, and you can ask her whatever questions you need to."

I glanced at the clock. Was his sister Dracula that she'd still be up in the middle of the night? Mark and I had only still been awake because of how his schedule sometimes worked as the only medical examiner for a spread-out county.

I waved Grady back to his seat. "Why don't you tell me why you think she needs my help, and then we'll talk to her in the morning?"

He crossed his arms again, reminding me a bit of a pouty little boy. "Tomorrow might be too late. If they bring her in first thing tomorrow, she might say something stupid. We need to go tonight."

Forget feeling like I'd made a deal with Rumpelstiltskin. I was starting to feel like I _was_ Rumpelstiltskin. In the TV show, he'd been controlled by a magical dagger. I was controlled by a promise I made.

I texted Mark to let him know where I was going.

Chicken, a voice whispered in my head.

I was a chicken. If I went to tell him in person, I was worried he'd be annoyed that I was heading out into the night. But Grady was waving my promise in my face, and if I didn't keep my word, what did that say about me?

Besides, I just wanted this to be over with. Odds were good I'd talk to his sister and find out Grady had been overreacting. Where that would leave us with our deal, I didn't know. I could probably make a good case that I'd fulfilled my promise at that point.

To my surprise, Mark texted back with *We did make a deal. At least once this is over, it won't be hanging over your head anymore. Be safe.*

I did love that man.

Grady insisted I ride with him. I would have argued except that I'd reached the point where I was probably too tired to be safe to drive myself back home.

He drove us through the center of town and out the other edge to a duplex on the outskirts of town. It was still technically within the town limits, but just barely. Fields started after the house beside it. The car in the driveway looked older than my elderly dog, Toby.

Grady shut off his car.

The drive here had been in silence since he hadn't seemed to want to discuss the situation, and I was too queasy to make small talk. I'd be glad when this stomach bug had found its way out of my system completely. Then again, it might have just been due to Grady's driving. He took the corners fast and sharp like he thought he needed to practice in case he ever found himself in a high-speed chase.

Now that we were here, though, I needed to know what he expected from me. "Should I wait here while you let her know what's going on?"

"I called her earlier about Lee. And if you stay here, I'll have to come back out into the cold to get you."

He got out and shoved his door shut.

Heaven forbid he have to be out in the cold more. He'd hauled me out of my warm house, when I'd been headed for my warm bed, into a night where my nose hairs froze.

But none of that was his sister's fault, and he was about to wake her up, too. I'd do what he wanted so everyone could get back to bed as soon as possible.

I trailed him up the driveway. He rang the doorbell twice, in a way that made me wonder if it was a signal or a pattern they'd established.

Faint light filtered through the patterned glass of the front door from somewhere deep in the house. A shadowy figure moved toward us, and the door popped open.

The woman on the other side wore a pale purple bathrobe. Her hair was pulled back in a ponytail, but one side was messed up and pulled loose. It seemed like my guess about the special way Grady rang the door had been right. Presumably had she thought she was answering the door for anyone else, she would have smoothed her hair back.

"Is it Mom?" she asked. "Why didn't you call?"

The look on her face said she expected the kind of news that you didn't give over the phone if you had any other choice. She obviously didn't connect our visit with Grady's earlier call about Lee Mills' remains.

Her gaze flickered in my direction, and her hands edged up to her hair. She pulled out her hair tie, letting her hair loose. "Who's this?"

Around town, everyone now called me Nicole Cavanaugh, but this wasn't a social situation. This was business.

I held out my hand. "Nicole Fitzhenry-Dawes."

The blank look that she gave me said my name didn't register, then something shifted. Her shoulders drew backward.

"You're that lawyer Grady's always complaining about hanging around the police station."

I swallowed down a snort of laughter. No surprise Grady hadn't spoken of me in flattering terms. "I've been involved in a lot of cases since coming to Fair Haven."

"She's obnoxious," Grady said. "But she wins."

The truly sad part of that description was that both my parents would have considered it a compliment. They'd rather be successful than liked. I wasn't sure that was the case for me. And, after all, shouldn't I be able to be both? Society definitely had a stereotype that liked to portray successful women as heartless witches. Or maybe it was the other way around—that there was the conception that women had to be that way if they wanted to succeed.

I had to hope and pray all that was smoke, mirrors, and lies. If it wasn't, Anderson had bet on the wrong person when he asked me to join him as a partner in his law firm. I wanted to win, but I wanted to still like who I was at the end of it.

Thankfully, I didn't care if Grady liked me at the end of it. He'd never liked me, and the feeling was more than mutual.

Hearing Grady's description of me had restored my sense of humor at least. It also restored a bit of my sense of freedom. I wasn't as much under his thumb as I'd originally felt due to the favor I owed him. He must have been desperate to come to me, given his opinions of me.

Grady's sister crossed her arms in a way that eerily mimicked Grady's favorite stance. "Why do I need someone who wins? I don't need a lawyer at all."

This was going to be fun if she was as much like Grady as this first impression was making her seem.

My ears ached from the cold. "Could we discuss it inside before I lose an appendage to frostbite?"

The quick look she exchanged with Grady felt like she was saying *You weren't kidding about her.*

I would have sworn the look he gave her back said *You have no idea.*

She stepped backward enough that we could enter. "Just be quiet about it. Gina's sleeping."

Her house felt sauna-warm after standing outside for so long. She pointed at where I could hang my coat, then led us into the living room. She took the armchair, sitting cross-legged. That left the couch for Grady and me. We took separate ends.

And then neither of them spoke.

To think I could have been home with Mark now.

Pull it together, Nikki, I admonished myself. *You're a professional, after all.*

A professional who'd learned my lesson when it came to not knowing my client's name. It'd gotten me into a pickle once when Elise tricked me into defending her ex-husband because I hadn't asked for the full name of the man she wanted me to defend.

I gave Grady's sister my best impression of my mom's smile—the one that gave every client who entered my parents' office confidence that she was the right choice. "How about you start by telling me your name?"

She glanced toward Grady, and I thought I caught an eye roll. "Geez. If you haven't even told her that much, what did you tell her?"

The affection in her tone when she spoke to him caught me off guard. From their first interaction at the door, I'd kind of expected that Grady's sister liked him about as much as I did. Now it seemed like she'd merely been caught off guard—and I couldn't blame her for that.

She focused back on me. "Daphne...Scherwin."

She added her last name belatedly, like she didn't want to risk any more vagueness.

I almost reintroduced myself, then realized how inane it would make me sound. "Your brother brought me here because he thinks you'll soon need a lawyer, but he wanted me to hear the story from you."

She closed her eyes and sagged slightly. She opened them again with a shake of her head. "I'm really sorry, but if he's brought you out here over Lee, he's wasted your time."

"Your boyfriend showed up dead." Grady's voice sounded like he was speaking around a clenched jaw.

"*Ex*-boyfriend, and the last time I saw him was twelve years ago."

Thanks to makeup, it could sometimes be difficult to guess a woman's age. Since we'd woken Daphne up, she wasn't wearing any. I'd have put her age somewhere slightly younger than me, which meant she would have been close to finishing high school when Lee Mills disappeared.

If there really was no need for me to be here, the sooner we established that, the better for me. "Do you know why Grady might think you'd need a lawyer?"

Daphne brought her shoulders up close to her ears and then lowered them down. It wasn't an I-don't-know shrug. It was more an I-don't-see-the-point shrug. "Lee and I had a public, nasty breakup, and his parents reported him missing the next day. Everyone assumed he'd run off to some big city somewhere the way he liked to talk about. 'More opportunities,' he always used to say."

She made air quotes around *more opportunities* in a way that made me think whatever Lee was talking about it hadn't been a hungrier job market. Presumably he wouldn't have talked to his girlfriend about romantic conquests that way. Mark had mentioned that the dead man was in the system because of petty crimes. Perhaps he was looking to move into bigger things that way, and he knew he couldn't do it in Fair Haven without being caught.

Daphne targeted Grady with a stare that would have shot laser beams at him if magical powers were a real thing. "I thought that's what happened when he disappeared. I told the police then—I didn't see Lee after our fight."

She'd obviously also told Grady.

With Lee's skeleton showing up still in Fair Haven, it was clear he hadn't gone anywhere. Daphne would be the first person the police questioned once they reopened the case. It wasn't surprising that an older brother would be concerned for her, but if what she said was true, she probably had nothing to worry about. Teenagers had messy breakups all the time. They didn't usually kill each other over it.

"Mom?" a girl's voice came from directly beside me, and I jumped.

I swiveled in my seat, but no one was there. A baby monitor sat on the end table. I could have sworn the voice belonged to an older child, but I must have been wrong.

Daphne unfurled her legs and got to her feet. "I have to check on her. Bottom line, I don't need a lawyer. Lee was alive the last time I saw him." She gave me a smile that missed her eyes. "I'm sorry he dragged you out here, Nicole. You weren't the obnoxious one tonight."

She hustled off into the house. Apparently, she figured Grady knew his way out.

I got to my feet, but he didn't move.

"So what's the next step?" he asked.

As far as I knew, the next step was he took me home. It was so late at this point that I didn't know whether to hope Mark was still up so we'd get a little time together or hope Mark had been able to fall asleep so he wouldn't be as exhausted tomorrow as I would.

I had a feeling, though, that Grady wasn't talking about taking me home. He might feel his badge gave him more importance than it did, but he hadn't struck me as stupid. When Mark and I needed his help last December, he'd actually been quite cagey in the way he went about it.

"I'm not sure what you mean."

He narrowed his eyes, as if he couldn't decide whether I was being intentionally dense or whether I was the stupid one. "With taking Daphne's case. Is there some paperwork we need to sign?"

"We have a contract for clients to sign, but unless *I don't need a lawyer* is code for the opposite, your sister isn't going to need to sign anything."

I internally cringed. I'd only meant to think that slightly antagonistic reply, not actually say it. But really, I couldn't be blamed.

Grady got to his feet. He didn't move toward me, but I felt the difference in our height and size. He'd probably intended me to feel it. When working with potential criminals, police officers had to come across strong and slightly threatening. "We have an agreement. You owe me a favor. Defending Daphne is it."

"I can't defend someone who doesn't want a lawyer. You can't sign for her." I headed for the front door. I might not be able to navigate without a GPS, but I could certainly find my way back to the front door myself. "Now, are you going to drive me home, or do I need to call Mark for a ride?"

Grady followed after me and clamped a hand down onto my coat before I could grab it from the hook. "She says she doesn't need a lawyer, but she will. I want your promise that you'll defend her when she does."

This was ridiculous. He was a member of the Fair Haven police. He knew Chief McTavish. He respected Chief McTavish, something that could be said of very few people where Grady Scherwin was concerned. Chief McTavish wasn't a man who went on witch hunts. He wasn't going to arrest Daphne simply because they'd been dating and had a fight the night Lee went missing. There would have to be more evidence than that before she'd need a lawyer.

After all, the police who'd interviewed her all those years ago hadn't felt they had enough to prove Lee hadn't simply run off. Even knowing he hadn't, if nothing back then had pointed to Daphne, it wasn't likely something now would, especially since she insisted Lee was alive the last time she saw him.

Grady's hand was still blocking me access to my coat, and it was too cold to go outside and wait for Mark without it. I glared at him.

The expression on his face lacked the confrontation I'd expected. The fire drained out of me and left a bit of an ache behind. He looked almost...scared. I'd been looking at him and seeing Grady Scherwin, badge-heavy police officer. Standing before me now was Grady Scherwin, worried older brother.

He might be a jerk, but just like with Ashley, that didn't give me an excuse to be one. I was the Christian here, after all. I should be kinder and more merciful even to people who weren't kind to me. "What makes you think she'll still need a lawyer?"

He lowered his hand to his side. His fingers twitched. "Because I know when my little sister is lying to me."

4

---

*T*he next day, Anderson watched me as I made my cappuccino from the fancy coffee machine he'd bought for our office. I'd been tempted to add a shot of expresso to it, but there was a fine line. I needed enough caffeine to keep me awake, but not so much that my heart raced like a hamster on a wheel.

Anderson tapped the side of my mug with his pen. "Are you sure you're not spreading yourself too thin between the two businesses?"

He didn't say *now that you're also married*, but I heard it. Anderson had never said so directly, but I knew he felt the best marriages were between people who worked in the same field because they often had similar hours and goals. He'd modeled his business after my parents, after all.

But I wasn't trying to be a superstar in even one of my businesses, let alone both. I was happy to simply do a good job. Besides, trying to balance married life with work had nothing to do with why I felt like all my energy had been sucked out with a straw and needed to be replaced by a caffeine drip. Mark and me living in the same house actually simplified my schedule.

I slurped down a too-hot gulp, leaving my tongue feeling like it was covered in fuzz. "It's not that. I got dragged out in the middle of the night by a potential client who was afraid she was going to need a lawyer."

Anderson slid his tablet closer. He tracked my legal schedule in it as well as his so we knew when each of us were available in case we needed to team up. "When's the bail hearing?"

I hadn't been entirely clear, so it made sense that he'd assume the only reason I'd go out in the middle of the night was if my client had actually been arrested. "The police haven't even questioned her yet. It was more precautionary. From what she told me last night, it's unlikely she'll even need a lawyer."

Anderson had a way of looking at me sometimes like he was channeling my dad. I secretly suspected he watched news footage of my dad in his spare time and practiced in front of a mirror. Though I might suspect that because practicing was how I had to work on maintaining a confident expression.

"You know what your dad would say about boundaries," he said.

I did. My dad would say that anything routine could wait for business hours because that way you kept yourself sharp for when it was most needed.

I warmed my hands on the mug but didn't risk a second sip yet. "I owe a favor." Grady and I hadn't discussed it, but I had a feeling he expected me to work Daphne's case for free as well. "And it's pro bono."

Anderson's expression and posture gave nothing away. He was too good a lawyer for that. Technically, we were supposed to discuss any pro bono cases before accepting them. It was part of our agreement.

"I'm sorry," I said. "They called in the favor unexpectedly, and I didn't want to wake you."

He slid the tablet out of his way. "That's okay. It'll happen sometimes."

I covered my smile with a hand. Anderson a few months ago might have been less easygoing about it. He had revenue goals for the business and big plans. I hadn't met his public defender girlfriend yet, but I had a feeling I'd like her.

A text made my phone shimmy on the table. I glanced at it.

Mr. Huffman signed the new papers, Tom McClanahan wrote. *I need you and Russ to come in and re-sign.*

Ugg, that made it sound like all the originals had somehow disappeared. Maybe I did need to talk to Tom about Ashley if that was the case. Just not now. Now I had enough other things to deal with.

"Sugarwood business?" Anderson asked.

"Nothing urgent." This partnership was ideal for me. It gave me the freedom to consult when Anderson needed me, but to only work a case myself when a client came in who claimed to be innocent. I didn't want to screw up the arrangement by having him think I wasn't committed. "It can wait."

Anderson collected up the papers. "That was the last item anyway."

He smiled, his teeth flashing extra white in his bronzed face. At first, I'd thought he did something vain like visit a tanning salon to stay so brown even in winter, but it turned out it was because he liked to ski and snowboard on weekends.

Anderson had originally hoped he and I might be a romantic match—before he learned I was engaged—but it never would have worked out even if I hadn't already been in love with Mark. A weekend on the slopes sounded like a great way to break a leg.

He tucked the papers into their folders. "I have a lunch date with Diana to get to anyway."

My phone rang before I could give him a teasing elbow nudge. I picked it up. The number wasn't Tom's office or Russ the way I'd been expecting.

"Nicole Fitzhenry-Dawes," I said.

"Chief McTavish brought Daphne in for questioning." Grady's voice was quiet and unnaturally calm, like he was trying not to let on that he felt anything other than confidence.

"That's okay." I slung my soft-sided bag over my shoulder. Once I disconnected with Grady, I'd call Russ. I could pick him up, and we could get the papers for the purchase signed this afternoon. "We knew they'd question her the way the police originally did because of her relationship with Lee and the argument."

"It's more than that," Grady said. "I'm in the middle of my shift, and the chief is sending me home."

That suggested that they were looking at Daphne as a person of interest rather than just double-checking the earlier state-ments. The chief didn't want Grady anywhere near the case because of his personal connection.

What I would never admit to him was that it was probably partly also because he'd crossed lines to help Mark when we needed it. While it'd been the right thing to do from the perspective of proving Mark's innocence and catching the real killer, Chief McTavish couldn't risk that Grady might violate the rules again to save his sister.

"Remember your promise," he said.

I remembered without him needing to remind me. Part of me balked at the strong-arming and the fact that he felt the need to exert control. He needed my help, but he also wanted to be sure that he remained the one in charge.

But I had promised, and it wasn't Daphne's fault that her brother didn't know how to interact with people as equals rather than as minions. "I'm half an hour away in White Cloud. If you can get a message to her, tell her not to answer any questions until I get there."

SHEILA WAVED AT ME FROM THE RECEPTION DESK BEFORE THE door to the Fair Haven police station had even closed behind me. Her wave was so big she looked like she was attempting to take flight.

Ever since Mark was cleared, she'd been trying too hard to act like nothing had changed between us. Things had changed. I knew now that I couldn't count on her to have my back. While I didn't blame her for looking out for herself, I also couldn't manage to pretend what had happened hadn't hurt me.

I lifted a limp hand in return and stopped in front of her desk. "I'm here as counsel for Daphne Scherwin."

Sheila jerked backward. Then she leaned in. "You know she's Grady Scherwin's sister, right?"

She whispered it, as if she expected me to back out once I learned the dirty truth about Daphne's identity. It wasn't a secret that Grady and I weren't best friends...or friends at all.

I wanted to tell her that Grady had shown loyalty to Mark and Chief McTavish and had helped us when we needed it most. All of that would have been true. It also would have been petty, rubbing it in that Grady—who I didn't even have a relationship with—had helped when she refused.

The fact that I thought about saying it meant I had more latent resentment to work through than I'd realized. It might be time to give my counselor a call again.

"Grady's the one who hired me," I said instead.

Her mouth formed an O shape.

Yes, Alice, you are in Wonderland.

She pressed a button on the phone. "I'll let the chief know you're here."

When Grady said Chief McTavish brought Daphne in for questioning, I'd assumed he meant it in a "royal we" sort of way, where Chief McTavish stood in for the department. It wasn't a good sign if McTavish chose to question her himself. He didn't usually go hands-on unless the crime was serious and he thought he had the perpetrator. Otherwise, Erik tended to handle interviews.

I'd mentally prepared to face Erik, not McTavish. It wasn't so much that I'd been banking on my friendship with Erik to earn me any leeway—Erik was too by-the-book for that. It was more that Erik never played dirty. McTavish would cut a suspect's heart out and set it on a plate so they could watch it beat if he thought it would get him the truth.

Dealing with an interrogator like McTavish required a different level of trust between a client and their lawyer. Last I spoke to her, Daphne hadn't wanted a lawyer. In fact, I wasn't entirely sure she even knew I was coming.

Joel Platten, Fair Haven's newest police officer, came to the front and escorted me back. My brain hadn't quite gotten used to seeing him there. It made me jump back to how many officers we'd lost in the past year. And how we'd lost them.

Even stranger was that he didn't know me. He didn't know my Uncle Stan when he was alive. He hadn't even grown up in Fair Haven. While that was likely the best for objectivity, it made for a quiet walk to the interview room. With almost any other officer, I'd have had a nice chat on the short walk. To Joel Platten, I was just another defense attorney—sort of the enemy.

I sneaked a glance at his impassive face. Maybe that was for the best, though. Maybe that was the mindset I needed. I was a criminal defense attorney. I could stand up to McTavish and protect my client.

Officer Platten opened the door into the interview room for me. Daphne wore a pink blouse and black dress pants that reminded me of a work uniform.

McTavish glanced up, and a quick frown ran across his fore-head. "Dawes. I didn't expect it to be you." He motioned toward the seat next to Daphne. "Or is it Cavanaugh now?"

"Fitzhenry-Dawes when I'm practicing. Cavanaugh every-where else."

I made sure to emphasize the *Fitzhenry* part. My mom was

just as good at what she did, and had played an equal role in who I was, as had my dad. McTavish just liked to cut my name in half because he found it a mouthful to say.

I couldn't read the expression on McTavish's face, but my ingrained lawyer instincts said he was trying to decide what he thought about the fact that I was keeping my maiden name for practicing law. My parents were nearly unbeatable in the courtroom. The impression that could make on McTavish could go one of two ways. He could think I wasn't a strong enough lawyer to make my own name. Or he could think I was trying to follow in my parents' footsteps.

I was going to hope he thought the latter.

Daphne's gaze switched between us. It settled on me in the end, with a look that asked *Are you really on my side?* I couldn't blame her. It was clear McTavish and I had a history, some of it friendly.

I touched a hand to her shoulder and took the seat next to her. "I know we're here because of the recent discovery of the bones of Lee Mills, but my client had nothing to do with his death. She already gave her statement to the police when Lee originally disappeared, and there's nothing new she has to add to that."

McTavish opened the file in front of him. A little chill crept into my feet and made my legs want to shake. The last time I'd faced McTavish in an interview room with a client, I'd made a miscalculation. He had information I didn't, and it made me look incompetent. For some reason, I couldn't help feeling like I was walking into another similar ambush this time. Daphne and I hadn't talked much. Almost everything I knew I'd gotten second-hand from Grady.

Grady, who thought his sister was lying about Lee being alive the last time she saw him.

But Daphne had insisted that Lee was alive when they parted ways, and she hadn't seemed to think she needed a lawyer. Gentle as a dove and wise as a serpent, the Bible said. I'd trust her unless she showed me I couldn't, but I'd also walk carefully where McTavish was concerned.

He flipped through the papers, and I waited silently.

He tapped his finger on a page as if he'd found what he was looking for. "In your statement, you told the police that the last time you saw Mr. Mills was outside of Hops. You two had a very public argument."

"That's right," Daphne said.

McTavish shifted his gaze, just enough for it to edge toward me.

Oh no. He'd expected I wouldn't let her confirm that statement. It was happening again. I was coming into this blind.

This was all Grady's fault. I shouldn't have let him push me the way he had. I should have insisted that I couldn't defend Daphne until she agreed. I should have done a proper intake interview with her first.

I dug my nails into my knees. As much as I wanted to throw something at Grady right now, I wanted to smack some sense into myself as well. This wasn't entirely his fault.

I should have insisted I be able to speak with my client before McTavish started the interview. I'd foolishly believed that she'd told me the truth last night when Grady and I showed up at her door. She might have lied to me last night because she hadn't thought she'd be considered a suspect this time around.

McTavish's gaze locked firmly on Daphne. "If that was the last time you saw him, then how do you explain the witness we have who saw the two of you together a few hours later?"

5

5

$\mathcal{W}$hatever else might be said of me, I tried to learn from my mistakes. Claiming to have a witness might be a bluff to push Daphne into confessing something. I wouldn't know how to proceed until I could ask her.

I held a hand up in the stop position. "I need a few minutes alone with my client."

Making the request would tip McTavish off to the fact that I wasn't sure whether he was bluffing or not, but it was better than being blindsided by what he planned next.

McTavish left the room, but he took the file with him. I'd partly been hoping to sneak a peek at it to see if there really was a witness.

The door whooshed shut behind him.

I angled in my seat. Daphne stared down at her hands instead of turning to face me.

"I think we can both agree you do need a lawyer," I said softly.

She nodded and shrugged at the same time. "I do, but I'll need a public defender. I looked up your name. There's no way I can afford you."

She'd likely found information on my parents. I didn't charge their prices. "No charge. I owe your brother a favor, and this is it."

She ran her nail along a crack in the table and nodded again. Whatever she was thinking, she wasn't the same woman as last night. The change made me think last night's air of nonchalance might have been an act.

"I have some rules that I require my clients to follow. I need the truth. I can't defend you if I don't know what I'm defending against."

She sucked in a long draw of air and blew it out so slowly I wasn't sure how her lungs could have held that much. "Outside of Hops wasn't the last time I saw Lee. We fought there, but he called me later to apologize. We met up afterward." She finally looked up at me. Her eyes were completely dry, but tightness pinched the edges of both her eyes and her lips. "I swear he was alive when I left him later, too."

We'd had an easy case to make when there'd been a restaurant full of witnesses who saw him drive away. We had a much more challenging task if someone saw them meet up again later, but no one saw Lee leave that meeting alive.

"Do you know if anyone saw him after you left the second time?"

She shot me a look that said she was contemplating a sarcastic comeback like *Other than the person who killed him?* The family resemblance to Grady popped to the forefront, across the gender divide—the cocky angle of her jaw, the set of her eyebrows above her eyes.

It vanished as quickly as it'd come. She dug at the crack again as if she wanted to dig all the way through the table. It made her seem younger than her age, like she'd gone back to that high school kid she'd been when Lee disappeared. "We were alone when I left him."

I wasn't my parents' daughter for nothing—I liked a challenge. I also liked to win, and this time the two might not go hand in hand. "We don't have much more time before Chief McTavish returns. Do you know who saw you together the second time?"

Her body turned slightly away from me. She probably didn't even know she was doing it. A shift like that was often a subconscious defense mechanism.

"I know exactly who saw us. Lee stopped to buy some beer. The guy who sold it to us saw me in the car. He even waved."

Had I been off about their ages? Daphne didn't look like she could have been over twenty-one at the time. That would make her older than me. But it was possible. Some people always looked younger than their age.

That wasn't the most important question I needed to ask in the few minutes we had left, though. "Do you have any idea why he would have lied about it back then and confessed to seeing you and Lee together now?"

Her hand moved to her throat as if she needed to convince the words to come out. "I blackmailed him to stay quiet. Lee and I were underage, and he sold to us all the time. I told him that if he spoke to the police about seeing us together, I'd tell them about his side business selling to minors. I told him if I ended up in prison, I'd take him with me."

A hairline fracture slithered through my trust in her. Blackmail wasn't an action of an innocent woman.

It might be the action of a panicked teenager, though, my logical side reminded me.

Teenagers weren't always the most rational. If she'd been frightened of the police blaming her for Lee's disappearance and she was innocent, she could well have done something to ensure more evidence didn't pile up against her.

At least she'd admitted it. And her admission answered why the witness spoke up now. Even back then, Daphne had exaggerated while blackmailing him. For a first offense, he probably would have gotten off with a fine and community service.

With how much time had passed, the statute of limitations was up. He couldn't be charged anymore. Daphne's old threat wasn't a threat now.

McTavish no doubt knew about the blackmail. And for all I knew, it wasn't the only additional piece of evidence against Daphne that he'd dug up.

If McTavish had anything else, I might not be able to get her out of here.

ot only did I not want to essentially lose this case so early, but I also didn't want to have Grady Scherwin banging on my door tonight, demanding to know why I wasn't able to keep his sister from being arrested.

When you run out of other options, my dad used to tell me, *stall.* You could find a way out of a lot of seemingly inescapable problems if you had a little more time.

McTavish came back in the door and dropped the folder onto the desk. It hit the table with a whap. "I hope you've convinced your client to stop lying to us."

I wasn't even sure I'd convinced her to stop lying to me.

I leaned forward and laid my arms on the table. "The only thing my client is guilty of is underage drinking. She lied because she thought she could still be punished for it now. I explained to her that wasn't the case, and so she willingly admits she and Lee Mills met up later for a few beers."

Daphne's chair creaked as if she'd shifted her weight. Crap.

There was definitely more she didn't tell me. She was a good enough liar to get away with it verbally, but not a good enough one to hide all her physical tells.

McTavish shifted his gaze to Daphne. I couldn't be sure if he'd seen her movement as well or if he was just going to continue to try to rattle her.

"If she lied to cover up a misdemeanor, why should I believe she wouldn't lie to cover up a felony?" he said.

I didn't glance at Daphne. I didn't have to. I couldn't almost feel fear radiating off of her like heat waves off asphalt in the middle of summer.

I rose to my feet. "Because she's a responsible mother with ties to the community. The fact that she was afraid of what a small infraction like underage drinking could do to her life now speaks to her law-abiding status." Some of the most vicious killers lived the life of a responsible citizen and caring spouse or parent on the surface. McTavish knew that as well as I did. He also knew that most juries didn't. They'd need more than vague accusations to be convinced that Daphne could progress from underage drinking to murder. I motioned to Daphne. "Let's go. There's no need for you to miss any more work today."

She peeked at me and then at McTavish as if she wasn't sure we could actually leave without his permission. No doubt she had an inflated view of what the police could do. Grady would have made sure of that to give himself an ego boost.

The look McTavish shot me suggested he was trying to figure me out. From our past interactions, he knew I only defended people I believed were innocent. And yet, if my client was innocent, why had I stonewalled him after my talk with her?

"Daphne," I said in a firm voice. "Time to go."

She slowly rose to her feet.

McTavish rose with us. "Stay available. I'm sure we'll have more questions as the investigation progresses, and I know you want to find out the truth about what happened to Mr. Mills as much as we do."

The sarcasm in his voice made me feel like a layer of grime coated my skin. I was used to working parallel to the police, seeking my own answers for a crime. I wasn't yet used to feeling like I was working against them.

I had to remind myself that I defended innocent people. Daphne claimed to be innocent.

I only wished I could change that from Daphne *claimed* to Daphne *was*, at least in my own mind.

I marched Daphne straight out to my car. Since she didn't tell me she had her own, I had to assume she'd gotten there some other way.

I waited for her to climb into my car and close the door. "I'm going to ask this once more. Did you kill Lee Mills?"

She shifted in her seat, and the seatbelt tightened across her chest as if it would force the truth out of her. "I didn't."

Her voice was solid, without a wobble or crack. She didn't sound nervous at all.

She also didn't quite meet my gaze.

Maybe that was why Grady thought she was lying. She might be telling the truth that she hadn't killed Lee, but she was also hiding something.

"Do you know who did kill him?" I asked.

She shook her head.

She might possibly be my least talkative client to date. I'd had clients who hid things from me before, but most of them still shared enough that I could catch the inconsistencies in their story. Daphne seemed to instinctively know that the less she said, the fewer chances she had of being caught in a lie. It was too bad the one thing she'd said earlier to Chief McTavish had been a lie.

I turned my engine on so we'd have heat. I didn't want to rush this conversation because I was cold. This was the drawback to having my office in White Cloud. Running my car this much wasn't good for my budget or the environment. I couldn't even blame Ashley for it this time.

"I need you to tell me what happened that night, in detail, so that we don't have any more surprises."

Daphne ran a hand underneath the seatbelt. "Lee was like a bad addiction that I couldn't kick. I met him when Grady and I were in separate foster homes, and I was feeling really alone."

I bit the inside of my cheek to keep from reacting. Had I made a guess about Grady Scherwin's past, I wouldn't have guessed he'd been in the foster care system. Maybe it explained a lot, though, about why he put so much emphasis on his position and status as a police officer.

Daphne let the seatbelt go. "Grady hated him. He thought Lee was making me do things I otherwise wouldn't have done."

I knew about the underage drinking. I could guess that another of Grady's complaints would have been sex. She was his little sister, after all.

For the first time in her story. Daphne met my gaze. The intensity of it felt like a slap.

"And before you ask," she said, "Grady didn't kill Lee. He worked six to six that night, and he had a partner since he was still new."

The fact that Daphne felt the need to defend him made me suspect him when I hadn't before. It was the opposite effect she'd been going for.

At least, I thought it was. Part of me couldn't shake the feeling that she was playing me somehow.

I nonchalantly raised my hands to the vents and let the warm air take the chill out. "So what happened that night?"

"The fight that everyone saw was because Lee cheated on me again. He called me later and apologized. Said I was the only one he cared about and it wouldn't happen again. He wanted to make it up to me."

She rolled her eyes like she'd been the stupidest person alive to believe him. I wouldn't have said stupid. I would have said young and desperately needing to feel loved.

"So you went?" I said.

She turned her face away from me. "So I went. He bought the beer, and we drove out into a corn field where we wouldn't be seen from the road."

I couldn't be sure, but I thought her neck flushed.

"We hooked up, and afterward Lee cracked open the beers. He got suspicious when I wouldn't drink any. He kept pushing until I admitted I was pregnant."

Her daughter, Gina. I must have been right when I thought the voice I'd heard over the baby monitor was from a child in their tween years. The baby monitor was kind of weird, but it was possible Gina was sick with the flu or Daphne had some other reason for it.

She'd paused long enough in her story that I could feel an unhappy ending coming.

She traced a line down the fog on the window. "Lee wanted me to get rid of the baby. He said we were too young to be parents—I was only seventeen—and he wasn't going to marry me just because I was knocked up. He even accused me of getting pregnant on purpose because his parents were rich."

Even after how much time had passed, her voice still carried a raw edge to it, like hearing those things said out loud again—even in her own voice—still hurt like the first time he'd said them.

"But I wasn't going to kill my baby." All the ache was gone from her voice, leaving only a coldness that sent a chill down into my core and would have convinced Chief McTavish she was guilty if he'd heard it. "We hadn't seen our loser dad in over ten years. Our mom couldn't stay out of rehab long enough to keep us. Other than Grady, that baby was the only family I had."

Grady probably wouldn't have asked me to take his sister's case if he'd known how much of his history I'd learn in the process. I wasn't sure how I was going to be able to look him in the eyes without him seeing a touch of pity there for what he and Daphne went through. My parents might have been emotionally distant, but they kept me safe and provided for every physical need, and I had my Uncle Stan. Thanks to him, I'd always felt loved.

Daphne gave a little shake-shiver. "I got dressed and left him there. It was the last time I saw him alive."

Did I touch her arm to show solidarity or not? How much like Grady was she? Any sign that I might feel sorry for him would make him angry and confrontational. I had to keep on good terms with Daphne if I was going to represent her. Reaching out to her might create a wedge.

But my mind kept replaying that part of the story where she went back to someone who'd betrayed her because he told her she was the only one he cared about. It spoke to such a deep level of need and self-doubt that it made my heart feel like it weighed more than my car. Even though it was years ago, I knew how the things we experienced in childhood stuck with us.

And, after all, she was Grady's sister, not his clone.

I put a hand on her shoulder. "I'm sorry."

Her muscles tensed under my touch. "Don't be sorry. Be a good lawyer. That's why my brother hired you."

I DROPPED DAPHNE BACK AT THE SWEET TOOTH, WHERE IT turned out she was the manager. I kept my car parked out front. Mark had texted to say he'd actually be home for supper tonight, so I wanted to be there, too. That meant I only had an hour or two to work on this case. McTavish was convinced Daphne killed Lee. It was only a matter of time until he felt he had enough to arrest her unless I could do something about it.

Grady wasn't likely to feel my favor was fulfilled until Daphne was cleared, and the last thing I wanted was to continue in his debt. With the start of a new year and my new life with

Mark, I wanted that old slate not only washed clean but sold to a new owner.

I'd tried to find out from Daphne who else might have known Lee was in that particular field that night or whether anyone else might have wanted him dead. She hadn't been able to give me an answer. She reminded me that she would have told the police about it when Lee originally went missing.

Usually when I worked a case, I had pictures of the scene or I could easily follow up on the victim's whereabouts. With a case so far in the past, even people's memories would be suspect. If someone asked me where I was or what I saw on a night over ten years ago, odds were good I wouldn't remember, either.

And as much as Fair Haven maintained an active and thriving rumor mill, rumors weren't something I could build a case on.

The best place to start seemed to be to identify the most reliable sources. Elise would have been off at school at the time, or at her first job, which I knew hadn't been in Fair Haven. Erik wouldn't have been here yet, either, and Mark would have been living in New York.

The only people I knew for sure were here and might remember any stories floating around about Lee's disappearance were Russ and Mandy. Russ had a policy about not telling me anything that wasn't a fact, and Mandy dealt in tall tales rather than truths.

I turned the radio on to the local Christian radio station and sang along for a minute. Sometimes forcing my mind to relax gave new ideas a chance to crawl out.

I needed someone who would have been aware of the case and the happenings around town at the time. I needed facts.

What I really needed was someone on the Fair Haven police force who'd been involved with the original investigation and was willing to talk to me.

Only one person might fit that description—Quincey.

I dialed his number and took my phone off of Bluetooth since I was parked. My phone had recently started dropping calls and cutting in and out when I was using a remote connection.

"Hey Nikki," Quincey answered. "Christine and I were just talking about inviting you and Mark over for supper some night next week."

Quincey's wife, Christine, made butter chicken that I dreamt about for days after. "I'll have Mark call Christine to set it up. I was actually calling on business this time, though."

I felt a little guilty asking him about it now. Since he'd opened with a supper invite rather than telling me he was at work, I'd gotten him on his day off.

"I wondered if Scherwin would try to hire you when the bones turned out to belong to Lee Mills."

For once, I couldn't blame the Fair Haven gossip hot line. Quincey probably learned all that from the source.

"*Hire* might be stretching it. I owe him a favor for helping us when Mark was arrested." I thought I heard Quincey chuckle, but it was faint enough that I got the impression he was trying to hide it. I could see how the thought of me working with Grady Scherwin would make anyone want to laugh. "Were you working here when he disappeared?"

"I was here, but I was only on the periphery of the investigation. What there was of it. Lee had a history of petty theft and vandalism. Most people thought he finally took off for a fresh start somewhere where people didn't prepare to call the police as soon as he stepped onto their property."

I never thought I'd hear myself think it, but I had to agree with Grady. If I'd had a sister, I wouldn't have wanted her dating Lee, either.

On the upside, a person like that was bound to have enemies. The question became whether we could narrow it down enough. I couldn't investigate a whole town or even all the people Lee might have wronged in his minor crime spree. "Did anyone he stole from or vandalized seem to want to take it further than calling the police?"

"I was the officer dispatched on one call where a business owner caught Lee with a can of spray paint. He ended up having to drop the charges against Lee in exchange for Lee dropping the assault charges against him. I'll text you his name."

I thanked Quincey profusely. Having him send me the name would save me the time of having to go digging through all the public court records.

Still, the police had likely already followed up on someone as obvious as that. It could quickly be a dead end. "Anyone else you can think of who might have wanted to hurt Lee?"

There was a pause, like Quincey was shaking his head and forgot I couldn't see him. "You should talk to Case Hammond, though. He'd been working as a dispatcher for about a year when Lee went missing. He's not much older than Lee and Grady, and I think I remember him knowing both of them back then."

Case Hammond. The man I'd tricked into giving me information when I was trying to build a defense for Mark.

At the police department's Christmas party that we attended right after returning from our cut-short honeymoon, Case had finally recognized my voice. An average person might not have, but it seemed to be part of his skill set as a dispatcher. Even though he didn't cause a scene, he made it clear that he knew what I'd done and what he thought of me as a person that I'd deceived him.

Of course, it wasn't enough that I was stuck in a favor to Grady Scherwin. Now I had to face Case again, too.

That meeting was not going to go well.

CASE HAMMOND DIDN'T ANSWER WHEN I CALLED. IF MY NAME showed up on his caller ID, he might never answer when I called.

I left a message, making sure to mention that I was legal counsel for Daphne Scherwin. He and Grady were friends, after all. He might not call me back otherwise, but he should for Grady's sake.

My phone dinged with a text. I moved it away from my ear to check it, and a low battery message blocked my view. Only five percent battery remaining even though I'd charged it to one hundred last night. It was either time for a new phone or a new charger. Unfortunately, I wouldn't be getting either this week. The nearest store that could figure out what was wrong was forty-five minutes away.

It was time for me to go home anyway. I wouldn't have time to follow up on any name Quincey sent me tonight, and I couldn't go running around without a phone. People had done it in the past, but I'd been in too many dangerous spots to ever feel safe again without a phone to call for help.

Mark's truck was already parked in our driveway when I pulled in. Near the tree line, the silhouettes of two people and either two large dogs or two miniature ponies headed away from me. Given the height difference between the two, it had to be Russ and Mandy walking my dogs before it got too dark.

Technically, *our* dogs now that Mark and I were married. I loved that we were an us, but it was still a little odd, like breaking in a new pair of shoes, no matter how much you adored them. Now it was our dogs. Our house. Our money. I felt the weight of trying to make sure I didn't let Mark down in some way.

Inside, I stripped off my shoes and coat.

Mark stood in front of the refrigerator, both sides held open. He shut the doors and turned around. "Is the food still in the car? I'll help you bring it in."

I'd taken cooking lessons from Mandy and from Mark's mom before we got married, but I was still far from domestic. Besides, when it came to the division of labor, we'd agreed to share things equally. I wasn't supposed to have dinner on the table when he came home unless it was my night to cook. I'd cooked last night, hadn't I?

"You look confused," Mark said. "Didn't you get my text? I asked you to grab a few things from the store on your way home."

I fished my phone out of my purse. I pressed the Home button, but the screen stayed dark. Apparently, five percent battery life didn't even get me fifteen minutes anymore.

I turned the black screen toward him. Even if he'd asked me to pick up takeout, I wouldn't have known. "Are we completely out of food?"

A smile drove Mark's dimples out of hiding. "Only if you wanted meat or vegetables. I think I spotted some just-add-water pancake mix behind the two remaining apples."

"I know we have peanut butter. I happen to like peanut butter and apples and pancakes, and I know we have plenty of syrup."

He opened his arms, and I walked into them for a hug and a kiss.

"I guess we need to schedule who buys groceries each week as well," Mark said when we pulled apart.

Mark mixed up the pancake batter while I washed and cut up the apples.

I kept having to stop myself from telling him about my day. I couldn't tell him about what really happened to Daphne that night. I couldn't tell him about calling Quincey and getting the name. I couldn't tell him about Case not answering my phone call.

It felt like I couldn't tell him anything. We were on opposite sides of this case. And for the first time, I wondered if Anderson wasn't more right than wrong that lawyers should marry other lawyers. Because Mark and I couldn't exactly spend the rest of our lives not talking about how we spent eight or more hours of every working day.

$\mathcal{M}$y call to Case Hammond the next morning went to voicemail again. Maybe he and Grady weren't as close as I'd thought if he wouldn't even take my calls for Grady's sake.

I might not even need Case, depending on what information I could find out from Royce Allen, the man Quincey said had a fistfight with Lee. It turned out he was the local plumber. He'd agreed to meet with me the following day at ten, which gave me time to run to the grocery store today.

If I didn't, we'd be down to eating the baking soda for supper. It was the only thing left in our fridge. We'd agreed to limiting how much we ate out. Even though we both made good money, we wanted to be responsible with it. Eating out seemed like a poor way to spend all our disposable income when so many charities could use it to help people or animals in need.

My trip to the grocery store even left me with enough time to drive to the nearest store that could diagnose my phone.

When I told Mark what was happening, he'd insisted I prioritize getting it fixed before I met with anyone who might possibly have been involved with Lee Mills' murder. I couldn't argue with his reasoning. With my phone's inability to hold a charge, I'd likely end up with a dead phone right when I needed it most.

The tech I dealt with said the problem was likely my charging port. He'd said it would take a few hours to fix, and I could either wait or come back the next day. Since I had a meeting with Royce Allen the following morning, coming back for it wouldn't work. Instead, I walked the mall for exercise and even picked up a present for Stacey's upcoming birthday.

Once I got my phone back, a third call to Case went to voicemail. He was definitely dodging my calls.

Mark and I were even home close enough to the same time that we were able to watch a movie together. It helped stave off the temptation to blurt out all my concerns about Daphne and this case to him. As hard as I tried, I couldn't help missing the days we worked cases together. Mark had a brilliant mind, and he'd often helped me make connections I wouldn't have made otherwise.

But maybe it was healthier for us to try to have conversations—heck, even entire evenings—where dead bodies and methods of murder weren't the main topic of our conversation.

ROYCE ALLEN'S TRUCK, PARKED OUT FRONT OF HIS BUSINESS, WAS powder blue, with a giant plunger painted on it along with the words *Go with the Flow Plumbing*.

His business catered to locals. Most of those didn't go with a punny name. Royce seemed to have decided he'd rather be memorable even if he was the only plumber in town.

The man who met me at the door wore coveralls in the same powder blue with the same plunger emblazoned across his chest. Royce knew how to brand himself even if it was so 1950s stereotypical that it made me cringe a little inside.

He'd probably been in his early thirties—a little over ten years older than Lee—when they'd gotten into the fight.

"You must be the lawyer," he said in the same way that someone else might have said *You have a rodent problem.*

I don't know why I expected anything different. A lot of people still made lawyer jokes even though they were long past being politically correct or acceptable in polite company. It just seemed hypocritical coming from a plumber. He wouldn't want me assuming he'd wear pants that created a plumber's crack when he worked.

Setting the judgmental attitude aside, it created a genuine problem. If he thought I was a scuzzy lawyer looking to cause trouble, I wasn't going to learn anything useful from him. He'd likely only agreed to this meeting because people often didn't realize they didn't have to speak to a lawyer, or even to a police officer, who came asking questions.

I hated to trade on Mark's name instead of on my own abilities, but in Fair Haven, his family had more influence than mine did. Or maybe I should say that his had more goodwill. Some people made the positive association between the *Dawes* part of my last name and my Uncle Stan, but more often people heard *Fitzhenry-Dawes* and connected it to my parents. They weren't just famous. They were infamous. They'd been a part of some of the highest-publicity criminal cases of the past ten years.

I stuck out my hand. "I practice law as Nicole Fitzhenry-Dawes, but my married name is Cavanaugh."

Royce shook my hand. His grip was surprisingly soft. "Grant Cavanaugh helped my family get through a real rough time when we lost my mother. You related to him?"

I didn't have to fake a smile. Grant and Megan made life easier for everyone who needed to say goodbye to a loved one. Even if Cavanaugh Funeral Home hadn't been the only funeral home in town, people still would have gone there.

"Grant's my brother-in-law. I'm married to his twin, Mark."

Royce moved out of my way so I could officially enter the building. Two tubs rested off to my left, and taps covered the wall to my right. Royce led the way back past a line of toilets and into an office.

Royce sat behind the metal desk that was wedged into the room so tightly it almost touched both walls. I took the only other seat—a stool that was hard for me to clamber up onto thanks to the heeled boots I'd chosen because they were my most professional-looking winter footwear.

"I'm not sure how much help I can be." Royce flipped over some papers as if it would be violating some plumbers code to have me see what fixtures his last customer had ordered. "I don't know anything about Lee Mills' disappearance. I wasn't even in Fair Haven the night he went missing."

A tingle crawled up my neck and into my face. He'd jumped to denial and an alibi faster than a completely innocent person would.

It put me in an even more difficult spot. By opening with an I-had-nothing-to-do-with-it statement, he'd ensured that all my questions would sound like I was calling him a liar. Calling someone a liar, in my experience, didn't tend to result in them telling you the truth.

There had to be a way around it. What did I really want to know from him—other than whether or not he'd been the one who killed Lee Mills?

Motive would be a good start. It was part of the trifecta of means, motive, and opportunity that were necessary to build a criminal case. The police already had two of the three against Daphne.

I crossed my legs. Doing so made me look more feminine, and that often tended to disarm men. "I heard that you and Mr. Mills had an altercation." I chose my words carefully. *Altercation* sounded less accusatory than *fistfight* or even *came to blows*. "I thought you might have known who else might have had a problem with him."

Royce opened one of the desk drawers. The desk shimmied. He swept the paperwork into it. "Throw a baseball out the window and whoever it hits could fit that description. Pretty much everyone in this town was happy to see Lee gone. The kid was nothing but trouble."

Adding the whole town to the suspect pool was worse than when only Daphne had been swimming around in it. "Could you give me some examples?"

He leaned back, and his chair squealed. Everything in his office seemed to need lubrication, including his tongue.

Calling on my natural naiveté about Fair Haven history

might convince him to narrow it down a little. The locals had been suspicious of me when I first arrived, but one thing that had helped was expressing my desire to become one of them. "I'm not from around here, so I'm still learning. Anything you could tell me to help me understand this case better would be appreciated. I feel like I'm playing catch-up because everyone else was here at the time."

Royce moved his lips back and forth in a motion that reminded me of someone swishing mouthwash around. "Lee was always destroying something or taking things that weren't his. He broke into Quantum Mechanics—Tony Rathmell's place—and smashed out all the windshields in the cars he had in for repairs. One time he hotwired Wayne Huffman's combine and took it for a joyride. Smashed it up enough that Wayne almost couldn't get his crop off that year." He leaned forward and rolled his chair closer to his desk. "Your other last name is Dawes. You related to Stan Dawes?"

I nodded.

"Lee and his girlfriend broke into that original sugar shack they had out at Sugarwood before the fire. Trashed the inside and left beer cans everywhere. That receptionist at McClanahan and Associates had her car broken in to by Lee."

That receptionist had to be Ashley, since Royce hadn't said the receptionist who used to work at McClanahan & Associates. The horrible, nasty part of me wished it had been Ashley who killed Lee. Not only would that spare Daphne and pay off my favor to Grady, but it'd stop Ashley from interfering with my legal needs.

I immediately sent up a prayer for forgiveness. Even if I

didn't like Ashley, I shouldn't wish prison time on her to make my life easier. Besides, even I couldn't imagine that Ashley would have killed someone over breaking into her car.

Royce continued with his list of names. I didn't recognize all the people on it, but I recognized enough of them that he hadn't been exaggerating when he said most of the town had been glad Lee vanished. He'd even stolen alcohol from Hops and cleared out the cash register at The Burnt Toast.

But Quincey hadn't mentioned any of those people getting physical. "What did he do to you?"

I kept my voice quiet and sympathetic, as if I were on his side. In some ways, I was.

Royce gripped the edge of his desk. "I came back after a middle-of-the-night emergency call and found him spray painting a steaming pile of—" He clamped his mouth shut as if he wasn't sure he was allowed to swear in front of a lawyer. "The police weren't doing anything to stop him. They kept saying there wasn't enough evidence to prove it was him. What they really meant was his parents had enough money to buy his way out of most of the trouble. I figured I'd teach him a lesson the old-fashioned way, and we'd all sleep better at night."

His eyebrows had come down over his eyes, and his voice held a dark edge. Had someone asked me when I first met him if I thought he was a killer, I'd have said that I couldn't see someone in powder blue coveralls with a smiling plunger on the front killing anyone. Now he reminded me more of an old-time gangster hiding behind a legitimate front.

He wouldn't have been the first person I'd dealt with who felt like they had to defend themselves because former Chief Wilson wanted to sweep everything bad under the rug to protect the reputation of the town and former dispatcher Henry McCloud took bribes to cover up crimes.

But Daphne wasn't the one who caused all the trouble. She shouldn't have to go to prison for something she didn't do, and the police didn't seem to be looking anywhere else but at her.

The problem was that Royce also seemed to have a temper under his unassuming exterior, and I didn't want it directed at me. I still hadn't gotten anything out of him that might help Daphne's case.

I shook my head slowly, sadly. "You took a big risk. The police could have thought that you came back and finished what you started by killing Lee."

He smiled at me. Actually smiled. Teeth showing. Eyes crinkling. "Karma. I stood up to a bully that no one else would stand up to, and I lucked out by being out of town when he was killed."

Out of town could mean a lot of things. If I was going to show that he had motive, means, *and* opportunity, I had to prove he was close enough that he could have driven back. "Where did you say you went again?"

I tried to phrase it as if he'd already told me and I'd forgotten.

His eyes tightened at the edges. "Florida. About as far away from here as you can get. I flew, too." He pinned me to my chair with a glare. "If you want my opinion, Lee Mills probably got a taste of his own medicine. Someone tried to steal his car, he thought he was a tough guy and could stop them, and they showed him otherwise."

If someone killed Lee over his car, if it was a random

carjacking with no other motive, then it would be almost impossible to figure out who killed him. Too much time had passed.

My mouth went dry enough that I couldn't help licking my lips. Maybe the car was the key to figuring all of this out.

The police originally thought that Lee had left town in his car. We now knew that Lee never left town. So where was his car?

It was possible Royce had done exactly that—Lee had been stealing from others and destroying their belongings, so Royce decided to see how Lee liked the same treatment and it got out of hand. I'd have to get our private investigator to look into whether Royce actually checked in for his flight or not. That was well after 9/11, when all the safety checks around flights tightened. If he hadn't checked in, there'd be a record of it.

Whether Royce turned out to be involved or not, the car was the key to figuring out what happened that night.

Royce pushed to his feet. "I've told you everything there is to tell. I've got another call to get to."

The look he gave me said that if I didn't get out fast, he was considering helping me leave. The man was a dormant volcano waiting for another chance to erupt.

I didn't want to let him know that I was afraid of him, though. Fear suggested I thought he was guilty of something. The last thing I wanted to do right now was tip my hand even more.

I rose to my feet, channeling as much of my mom's decorum as I could. Somewhere in my body, I had to have that gene, right? Even if it was recessive.

I extended my hand to Royce. "Thank you again for your time. You've given me a lot of people to follow up on."

Royce took my hand, but when I went to finish the handshake, he refused to let go.

"Just remember that the people you're looking into are good people. The bad guy is dead, and no one cares what happened to him."

My hand went numb for a reason other than that Royce seemed intent on cutting off my circulation. He thought I was working with the police—that I was with the district attorney's office. That's why he'd felt he needed to meet with me. "I'm Daphne Scherwin's defense counsel. I'm interested in defending her, not in hurting innocent people for the sake of a guilty one."

He released my hand. Something flickered across his face that I couldn't interpret. And I wasn't going to stick around to probe further. I wasn't in danger, but I was sure Mark would have said I shouldn't have come alone anyway.

It took every ounce of my self-control to turn my back on him and mosey away like my insides didn't feel like they were trapped inside a blender.

I climbed into my car and let the seat do the work of holding me up. I'd promised Daphne that I'd call her with an update today. I hadn't expected to have much to update her on, but my parents had always taught me that frequent communication with clients kept them calm and helped prevent them from doing anything stupid.

Before I called her, I wanted to check in with the police and see if they were searching for the car. It would give me something concrete to tell her.

I dialed Chief McTavish's number, but my phone beeped in my ear. No signal.

Fair Haven's infamous cell phone dead zones likely couldn't even be blamed this time. My phone was on its last breaths of life.

While I wouldn't feel comfortable facing Royce in a dark alley, he wasn't going to hit me over the head in broad daylight. I crawled back out of my car and wandered around the parking lot until my phone picked up a signal on the far side of Royce's truck. For a man who hustled me out of his store because he had an urgent call to get to, he was slow off the start.

I dialed Chief McTavish's cell number.

"If you can't reach your husband, it's because he's out at the edge of the county. A transport crossed the center line."

I pulled the phone away from my face and squinted at it. I'd called McTavish's number, and it was his voice, but that had to be the weirdest way to answer I'd encountered yet. Mark had texted me that he was headed out of town, and it wasn't like I expected to be able to keep tabs on him all day anyway. We both had our own work to do.

"I wasn't calling to find out where Mark is."

Muffled voices came from the background, as if someone had joined McTavish and he'd covered his phone with his hand.

I waited.

"I couldn't think of another reason," McTavish said when he returned, "for the lawyer of a person of interest in an open investigation to be calling me."

Ahh. I got it. Chief McTavish had been a member of Internal Affairs for years. His final assignment for IA was what brought him to Fair Haven. He'd asked to be allowed to stay on as Fair Haven's chief of police because his wife was tired of moving and being unsure of who she could trust. All those years of making sure other police officers hadn't crossed the line meant he kept the line for himself drawn in concrete.

The only way to remove a line from hardened concrete was with acid or a jackhammer. I didn't want to take either of those nuclear options with McTavish. We needed to maintain a good working relationship. For my future clients' sakes, and for Mark's. I'd already made things confrontational enough during Daphne's interview.

Still, finding that car was crucial. He might not tell me anything, but by asking, I'd at least plant the idea in his head. "I know there's not much you're able to tell me, but I was hoping you could confirm you're looking for Lee Mills' missing car."

Silence filled the other end of the line. I used to think Erik was married to procedure. That was before I met McTavish.

I could hear him breathing, so I knew he was still there and the silence wasn't because my phone had died. Yet.

"Fine. You don't have to tell me anything. Please just look for the car if you're not already. If you can find out what happened to it, I think we'll find out what really happened to Lee."

"I'll take that under advisement," McTavish said. "Goodbye, Ms. Fitzhenry-Dawes-Cavanaugh."

He disconnected, but I could have sworn I heard a smile in his voice before he did.

I turned around to head back to my car and stumbled to a stop.

Royce stood by his front bumper. He'd heard everything.

8

*C*rap. Crap, crap, and double crap. If Royce had anything to do with Lee Mills' death, I'd now given away my advantage. He knew I was hunting for the car, and he knew I wanted whoever I'd been talking with to hunt for the car. He ran his own successful business, so I had to assume he was a smart man. He'd be able to guess I'd been talking to the police.

I waved at him and strode past like I didn't care if he'd overheard me or not. "Have a nice rest of your day." I added an extra dollop of cheerful to my voice.

I still owed Daphne an update, but I wasn't going to stand around Royce's property and give it to her. I'd given away enough already.

I drove down the street and parked in the parking lot for the shopping center that housed the optician, dentist, and chiropractor's office. I'd always found it ironic that Fair Haven had an optician—who could sell and fix glasses—but not an optometrist —who could tell you that you needed them.

I entered Daphne's cell number.

"Hello?" Daphne's voice said.

"It's Nicole. Is now a good time to talk? It won't take long."

"Nicole? I can't hear you. You're cutting in and out."

I was sitting still, and my phone showed plenty of service bars. The tech had clearly been wrong about what the problem was. "I was just calling to update you."

"I can't hear you. I'm at home. You could try the land—"

I checked my phone screen. Even though I hadn't moved, my phone had lost the signal completely. You had to be kidding me. That was it. This phone had to go.

Daphne's duplex was along the route I'd take to head to the town where I could buy a new phone. I might as well stop on my way by.

A second car took up the space in Daphne's driveway when I pulled up. It wasn't Grady's. I'd seen him coming and going from the Fair Haven police lot enough times to recognize his personal vehicle. The one sitting behind Daphne's car did look a bit familiar, though.

I rang the bell.

Daphne opened the door. "What are you doing here?"

Even though my update wouldn't take long, I did want to ask her some questions about Lee's car. I could have our firm's private investigator see what he could find, along with looking into Royce's travel records.

My questions, however brief, would take too long for me to do from the front steps. I was already starting to shiver.

"We need to talk about your case." I inclined my head. "Inside."

Daphne glanced back over her shoulder. "It's not a good time. I had to take Gina to the ER this morning for an infection, and she really needs quiet to rest."

She made it sound like I was bringing a marching band inside with me.

I stopped a second before looking back over my shoulder at the second car. Doctors didn't make house calls even in Fair Haven. She didn't want me to meet whoever was in the house with her.

"I'll be quick and quiet, but it can't wait." I patted my pocket. "I tried to call, but my phone died."

Daphne backed up one slow step at a time. I lunged through the door and dropped my coat and shoes before she could change her mind.

Case Hammond rounded the corner. "Who was at the—" His gaze landed on me, and he cursed.

This was the last place I'd expected to find Case Hammond hiding from me. "I guess that confirms that you were avoiding my calls on purpose."

He moved over next to Daphne. "You don't have to let her in even if she is your lawyer. I told Grady she'd stick herself into parts of your life that had nothing to do with the case. He didn't listen to me."

Seriously. He acted like I'd hung his boxer briefs up on the station flag pole. All I'd ever done to him was pretend to be a secretary in distress who was afraid of getting in trouble with her boss. Actually, when I thought about it, it was a bit of a slimy move. He could have gotten in trouble for it. Given the state of things at the time, if no one believed his story, he could have been fired or arrested.

Daphne clapped her hands once, sharply. Both Case and I swiveled to face her.

"Keep your voices down or I'm kicking both of you out." Her words came out with a hiss to them.

She had said her daughter was sick and resting. Now I felt like an even bigger jerk. Case was already apologizing.

Daphne raised her hand, and he stopped. "I'm not going to referee you two the way I have to Grady and my mom. I'd like you both to stay, but I can't take the stress of more bickering." Her voice cracked on the end.

She was right. My parents would have suspended me for acting that way in front of a client. It didn't matter how Case acted. I had to remain professional. There was no reason for me to get overly emotional like this.

"I'm sorry, too," I said. "If you're still willing, I have a couple of things I need to discuss with you about the case. I think I have a lead that will help prove that someone else killed Lee."

Daphne led the way into the living room. Case followed along behind her, his hand up at her back level but not touching her. It spoke to a familiarity, but also told me they weren't in a romantic relationship. If they had been, he would have placed his hand on her back.

Daphne didn't offer me anything to drink even though two mugs sat on the coffee table. She and Case had been having a cup of tea or coffee together before I arrived. Empty plates dusted with crumbs suggested they'd also eaten lunch together.

I perched on the edge of the couch. Hopefully that would reassure her that I didn't intend to stay long. No sounds came from the nearby baby monitor, so at least our earlier argument hadn't woken her daughter after all.

Case sat in the arm chair, but Daphne stayed standing.

I folded my hands in my lap. "I'm following a lead on Lee's car. I think that if we can find it, we can find the person who killed him. Can you remember any details about it? The color? The model? The license plate?"

Daphne's gaze shifted in Case's direction. It was so slight I might have imagined it. "It was red." She brought her shoulders up, but they were almost too tight to be considered a shrug. "I'm not a car person. I can't say more than that."

Knowing the car was red would have helped if someone brought a red car in to be repainted, but I couldn't exactly have Hal, the firm's private investigator, calling all the body shops in the area to check their records for whether someone brought a red car in to be repainted over a decade ago.

If Daphne couldn't tell me more about Lee's car, maybe his parents could. "Do you have the contact information for Lee's parents? They might be able to give me the details I need. It would help to talk to them anyway about that night and what they might remember."

"Can't you just read their statements?" Daphne picked up the plates from the coffee table. They clinked together. "They would have told anything they knew to the police already."

It sounds like she doesn't want you talking to Lee's parents, the suspicious voice in my head that sounded like my dad said. I ignored it. My dad thought everyone was guilty. At first, he'd even implied Mark was guilty when he'd helped with his case before our wedding. It was more likely she didn't want me bothering them when they were mourning the loss of their son all over again.

I'd be respectful of their grief, something Daphne didn't know. Since I'd started this case, I'd been a bit like a bull chasing the clowns around a rodeo ring—aiming at everything that came close to me whether it was the target I should be chasing or not. It wasn't like me. I suspected it was because I felt the stress of knowing Grady expected certain results from me and my frustration at not being able to work the case with Mark. Neither of those gave me an excuse for being bossy, pushy, or unkind, though.

There was a balance in there that I needed to find between getting things done and still being the person I wanted to be at the end of it. I could find that balance. Daphne didn't have to feel the need to protect Lee's parents from the insensitive lawyer.

"I can't access any of the past evidence because the police haven't officially arrested you. They won't give me anything until then, and I'd like to avoid you being arrested in the first place."

This time Daphne looked at Case without trying to hide it. She set the plates back down on the coffee table. She moved toward Case, and for a second, I thought she was going to sit on the arm of his chair. Instead, she passed by and settled on the end of the couch, as far away from me and as close to Case as possible.

"Lee's parents might not talk to you." It was Case who finally spoke.

Unless Lee's parents were behind what happened to him or they were protecting another one of their children who might have hurt Lee, there was no reason for them to be hesitant to speak to someone who only wanted to uncover the truth about what happened.

I gave Daphne my most reassuring smile. "I'm sure they'll want to help if it means finding their son's killer."

"They won't." Daphne leaned forward and wrapped her arms around her knees. "Not if they know you're my lawyer."

An uncomfortable feeling grew in the pit of my stomach like I'd eaten something that wasn't going to agree with me. That sounded an awful lot like they thought Daphne was involved.

But if that were the case, why didn't they tell the police that back when Lee disappeared? Quincey would have heard about it if they had, and he would have told me.

I was back to feeling like Daphne only shared what she felt she absolutely had to. "I know that you don't want me poking around in your personal life." I shot a glance at Case. "But a criminal defense attorney is like a doctor. Your doctor can't help you if you hide symptoms or don't give him the whole picture. I can't protect you if I don't know what's going on. It turns me from a doctor into a fireman, and no matter how quickly firefighters get to a scene, there's always some devastation."

Daphne rubbed her hands along her shins. Her gaze shifted to Case. Something passed between them that I couldn't read. Like a silent conversation.

She must have seen what she was looking for because she sat up.

"Gina has sickle cell anemia. We found out when she was six months old. Up until then, Lee's parents were a huge part of her life, babysitting while I worked even. After the diagnosis, they cut us out."

The sick feeling in my stomach rose up into my chest. No wonder Lee was the way he was if his parents had made his acceptance conditional upon perfection. I knew what feeling like you had to earn love did to a person. It either turned you into an overachiever or a rebel. I'd chosen to try to go one way. Lee had chosen to go the other. If his parents were going to think he wasn't worth anything, he might as well prove them right.

I might be laying my own experience on top as a template when I shouldn't, though. "You're saying the Mills rejected Gina because she was sick?"

"Because she was sick with a genetic disorder, and no one in their family had it. I tried to tell them that she got it from my side. It runs in my family. My uncle had it. That wasn't good enough. They said Gina couldn't be Lee's daughter."

Good thing I'd checked. I had made a wrong assumption about their motives.

It was still a sad situation. Once they decided Gina wasn't their granddaughter, they might also have suspected Daphne killed Lee for whatever reason.

"Has a paternity test been done?"

Daphne shook her head. "If they wouldn't take my word that Lee was Daphne's dad, then we didn't need them. Grady helps out, and so does Case."

Case was either a really good friend or something else was also going on here. Based on the way they seemed to want to be closer than they were, I suspected they had feelings for each other that they hadn't shared yet.

Case leaned on one arm of the chair. "My older brother has sickle cell, so my family knows what it takes."

It was almost like he'd seen the thought wheels turning in my head and wanted to give me an explanation before I came up with one he wouldn't like.

His explanation had one odd point to it. "Your whole family helps out?"

The muscles in Case's arms flexed like he'd subconsciously tensed them. "My parents were Grady's foster parents. They were trying to get Daphne, too, to let them be together, until my mom passed away. Then my dad had all he could handle already with my brothers and me and Grady."

The sick feeling in my chest turned into an ache. When I'd tricked Case to get information to help Mark, I'd banked on the fact that Case had a rescuer mentality. At the time, I'd based that guess on his friendship with Grady, assuming his machismo would make him want to save a woman in distress.

I'd been right about the need to rescue, but I was starting to think I was wrong about its source. A man whose parents had fostered and who grew up with a sick brother would have learned to take care of people. He'd been raised to do it, and it had nothing to do with his view of women.

"Do you know if Lee's parents ever told their suspicions to the police after Gina's diagnosis?" I asked.

Daphne shook her head, and Case shrugged. It would have been a footnote at the time if they had. Chief Wilson wouldn't have dived back into a cold case. It could explain why Chief McTavish was so focused on Daphne now.

I might still give Lee's parents a try. Even if they were hostile, I'd learn exactly why they suspected Daphne over anyone else. Getting pregnant by someone other than your boyfriend wasn't a reason to kill your boyfriend.

I got to my feet. "Thanks for..." They hadn't really helped with the case. "For sharing that with me. I'll still try to contact Lee's parents. The worst they can do is refuse to talk to me."

I cringed internally. That could be taken as a dig at Case. He didn't respond, so hopefully he hadn't taken it that way.

It still seemed odd that he wouldn't have returned my calls, but it was likely as simple as him wanting to protect Daphne and Gina from someone he saw as being more harmful than helpful.

My phone gave off a strangled imitation of my regular ring tone, almost like it didn't have enough strength for the full thing. I glanced at the screen.

Mr. Huffman.

That was a call I needed to take. Russ was anxious to get things moving on planting the trees, and the police had finally released the field.

At first it'd seemed strange that Russ wanted to expand Sugarwood. Sugar maples took forty years before they could be tapped. He'd never see these trees come to maturity. I'd be retired before anyone harvested their sap. But Russ said that was the beauty of a sugar maple bush. It was generational. My children could keep it going along with Stacey and baby Noah, since Russ planned to leave his share of Sugarwood to them.

I waved at Daphne that I'd see myself out and answered the call.

"Ms. Dawes-Cavanaugh?" the man's voice on the other end of the line said.

Great. Apparently being married wasn't going to make my last name easier. It was just going to give people new ways to mangle it. "This is Nicole."

"I need to talk to you about the sale of my field. Today."

hrough my ragged cell reception, I arranged to meet Mr. Huffman at The Burnt Toast Café since he couldn't make out half of what I was saying over the phone. Daphne came up to me during the call and put a finger to her lips to remind me to be quiet. I must have been shouting to try to get Mr. Huffman to hear me.

I certainly wasn't winning points with anyone today. With the way things were going, Russ would call next and tell me that all our saplings had died because I didn't get a voice message that told me I needed to water them.

At least meeting at The Burnt Toast meant I could get myself a cup of coffee and something sweet. The Burnt Toast carried cannoli that I loved. If I had time, I could try to talk to the owner, Mr. Dobson, about adding a maple syrup mousse to their menu. I'd gotten the idea after eating a delicious mousse on my honeymoon. The Burnt Toast already used our maple syrup for their breakfast items, but expanding our products into new venues was one of our long-term goals.

That was assuming I had the heart for another business discussion after I talked to Mr. Huffman. If he sold his farm to someone else, we wouldn't be able to expand Sugarwood—ever. The other three sides of the property butted up against roads.

We had a deal, though. He shouldn't be able to back out of the sale now. I assumed property law worked similarly to other kinds of law where being in breach of contract landed you in court.

Mr. Huffman wasn't there when I arrived, so I placed my order and made the call to Hal. The restaurant was so busy and my connection was so terrible that I had to give up before I could make him understand what I wanted. I didn't want to try shouting. The last thing I needed was everyone in Fair Haven knowing I was investigating Royce Allen and Lee Mills' missing car. Shouting hadn't worked with Mr. Huffman anyway. I sent Hal a text with my request.

I'll need more info on car, Hal replied.

Contact Lee Mills' parents, I texted back. It might be better if Hal contacted them anyway. The more degrees of separation from Daphne, the more likely they were to answer—or, at least, that's what it had sounded like.

I'd barely received his affirmative reply when Mr. Huffman showed up. He had on thick tan winter coveralls, as if he'd been working outside before he called me and hadn't bothered to change. He took off his winter hat and laid it on the table. The hat was red and bore a seed company logo, the little white pom-pom on top held on by a thread.

Mr. Huffman shook my hand. "I've never liked to have important conversations over the phone anyway. Maybe I'm old-fashioned, but I think it's better to talk face to face."

That was a mindset that seemed to be vanishing with every new generation. I still liked in-person conversation because I struggled to read people over the phone. For the generation after me, even email was fading in popularity. Stacey Rathmell, who co-managed Sugarwood, texted people more than she called them.

He patted his thin hair, but strands stuck back up after he moved his hands away, the static electricity left behind by his hat giving them a life of their own.

"The thing is," he said, "I need to know if you're serious about this sale."

He'd mentioned another offer before. Had they increased it? We already had paperwork signed, but I'd feel bad if he could have gotten a lot more money for the property. I'd have to talk to Russ about it and see what we could do if that was the case.

My dad would tell me not to let on that we needed him more than he needed us. I didn't want to operate that way in this case. I wanted the deal to be fair to everyone, and I had to believe that Mr. Huffman would value my honesty. He seemed to care about who got his land next and how they planned to use it. He didn't want to sell to a faceless corporation.

The waiter set down our orders. Mr. Huffman's coffee had so much cream in it that he might as well have ordered a latte. At least then his drink would have still been warm when it arrived. I waited for the waiter to leave again.

"We're very serious," I said. "Your field gives us our only

chance to expand. Sugarwood hasn't been in my family long, but I hope it stays in my family long after I'm gone. I want to leave my children the best possible setup."

At the mention of children, he started nodding his head along with what I was saying. "It's about family for me, too." He placed his hands flat on the table. "With all the mix-ups about the paperwork before and now you refusing to sign the new documents…If you've changed your mind or can't get the money, I just need to know. My wife and I don't have retirement savings or a pension. All we have is what we'll get from these sales. We need to sell."

Refusing to sign the documents?

Oh no. Tom texted me that the documents were ready days ago, right before Grady called me that Daphne had been brought in for questioning. With the case and my sickly phone, I'd forgotten all about it.

I tucked my hair behind my ears. After all the delays around this sale, I couldn't blame Mr. Huffman for wondering what was going on.

"I've been busy at work, but I promise I'll go today and get them signed." I held out my hand for us to shake on it. "You have my word."

He shook my hand, but his grip wasn't as firm as the first time. "I hate to push. It's just that we've barely gotten by without losing the two farms. When the crops were bad or my machinery broke down, we had to take out loans. At one point, I was out every night trying to keep kids from driving through the fields because we couldn't afford even that small loss. My wife never even got a honeymoon or a vacation that didn't involve staying with relatives. Selling now means we can pay our debts and live out our golden years with dignity."

My Uncle Stan and Russ had managed Sugarwood well enough that we had reserves to see us through a bad year. But they had both been good businessmen, and Stacey was shaping up to be a good businesswoman. Not everyone had those skills. If the crops produced a low yield, a farmer could easily go under.

I couldn't imagine living under that kind of pressure for so many years, only to then have to worry about the bottom falling out of the land sale when the time came.

I hadn't realized the personal implications for him. "I'll go right now."

He tapped the table next to where the waitress had set my order. "Finish your food first and talk a little shop with me. What's been keeping you so busy?"

There wasn't too much I could tell him that wasn't confidential. Hopefully he didn't think I was being rude when I didn't offer details. "I've been retained by Daphne Scherwin as her defense counsel. The police have been questioning her about the death of Lee Mills. His bones were the ones my dog found on your land."

Mr. Huffman looked a little queasy at the mention of the bones. He'd said he used to hunt, but there was a difference between seeing the bones of an animal and seeing the bones of a human being.

He chugged the last of his coffee. "That's good. Whoever killed that boy probably had a decent reason. I was always surprised no one decked him before Royce Allen took a swing at him. Maybe if more people stood up to him sooner, stopped him, he wouldn't have ended up the way he did." He held up his coffee mug in the direction of the waiter, indicating he'd like another cup. "But I meant I wouldn't mind hearing all your plans for expanding your bush. I get enough murder stories from those *CSI* shows my wife watches on TV."

ANOTHER HALF AN HOUR PASSED BEFORE MR. HUFFMAN AND I parted ways. The pace of life in Fair Haven had always been slower than in DC, but Mr. Huffman came from a generation where you didn't do your business and run. You got to know the people you were doing business with.

I liked it. It made me think of how I wanted to get to know my clients, not only because I could mount a better defense for them, but also because I always wanted to see them as people first. Mr. Huffman liked to know the people he was doing business with because he could trust them more.

By the time we finished, it was too late for me to stay around and talk to Mr. Dobson. McClanahan & Associates would be closing in half an hour, and I'd promised to sign the papers today. Russ had probably been there the same day he was asked.

We parted ways at the door, and I climbed into my car. I put on my signal to indicate my intention to pull out of my parking spot and checked my mirror.

Something black was scribbled all over it. How had that happened? I hadn't driven close enough to anything to get something on it, and it didn't look like anyone had hit it.

If a police officer saw me driving with my mirror that dirty,

I'd be pulled over for sure. I dug a leftover fast food napkin out of my console and rolled down my window.

The black squiggles were words.

My head felt like I'd accidentally bumped it into a shelf, and my eyes didn't want to focus. Words written on my mirror couldn't be good. No one wrote anything good on another person's car mirror.

I closed my eyes and took two deep breaths. I had to see what they said. I couldn't sit here forever.

I forced my eyes back open.

Stop looking for the car, someone had written in what looked like permanent marker. *Even a cat only has nine lives.*

10

*M*y hand instinctively reached for my phone to call Mark. My fingers made contact, but I stopped before dialing. I shouldn't be calling anyone on that phone. Mark would only hear every other word, and he'd probably think I'd crashed my car again or something even worse.

Besides, he'd said he would be doing an autopsy today. He probably couldn't even answer his phone right now. And what could he do about it other than comfort me and then worry about me and want me to do exactly what the message said and stop hunting for Lee Mills' car?

Because history had proven that people who sent threatening messages to me tended to try to carry out their threats.

I jammed the close button for my window so forcefully that my finger ached. Anderson and my parents didn't get threats like this. Was it because they were more intimidating? People were scared to threaten them, but they saw me as weak?

It's because they defend the bad guys, my logical side said. *Anderson and your parents aren't a danger to them. You are.*

Which made sense. It didn't make me feel much better about the fact that I'd received yet another threat, but it made sense.

I definitely wasn't getting a new phone today. After I fulfilled my promise through a quick stop to McClanahan & Associates, I had to head to the Fair Haven police station. If Chief McTavish wasn't taking my lead about the car seriously before, he'd have to now.

Whoever had left that message on my window had made a serious mistake.

I PULLED UP THE PICTURE I'D TAKEN OF MY WINDOW AND HANDED my phone to Chief McTavish.

I scooted my chair closer to his desk. "Royce Allen overheard me call you about the car. It might have been him. But I was also talking to my private investigator about it while I was sitting in The Burnt Toast. Someone might have overheard me. We'll know for sure once we find the car. There has to be something about it that points to Lee Mills' murderer."

My words came out in more of a rush than I'd intended. I'd planned to come in and present the picture as a calm professional. I hadn't counted on the fact that the fear-and-excitement cocktail surging through me would make me act a little more like I'd had a few real cocktails.

Chief McTavish looked up from my phone. "You're the only

person I know who gets a threat and pushes harder in that direction rather than backing off."

Chief McTavish had often accused me of lacking common sense. I ended up in situations no normal person would.

To me, that didn't say I lacked common sense. It meant I cared enough to find the truth even if it put me in harm's way. "That's because if someone wants me to stop looking, I know I was looking in the right direction."

Chief McTavish's mouth twitched like he wanted to smile but wouldn't give me the satisfaction. "I've always thought threatening letters were a miscalculation on the criminal's part." He pushed my phone back across the desk. "We're doing what we can to find the car, but it was probably torched or broken down for parts years ago."

I took one more peek at the picture and then slid my phone back into my purse. McTavish had a point. And yet, if whoever killed Lee knew his car could never be found, why were they afraid of me looking for it?

"Will you bear with me on a theory?"

McTavish leaned back in his chair and crossed his arms, but he didn't say *no*.

"They wouldn't be this worried if they were sure the car was destroyed." I spoke slowly. My idea was only half formed, and I needed time to bring it all together as I laid it out for Chief McTavish. If I got it wrong or sounded illogical, he'd send me away, and I didn't have the resources to do the kind of search necessary. Hal could only find it if it were someplace fairly obvious. "That means the last time they saw the car, it was whole. When I talked to Royce Allen, he said—"

Chief McTavish cleared his throat in that way that said *You're wrong, and I'm going to stop you there rather than letting you go on.* "We know about Mr. Allen's fight with Mills shortly before Mills' death. But we checked his alibi. He flew to Florida two days before and didn't return until four days after. He couldn't have killed Mills or disposed of his car."

I barely kept myself from exclaiming *what?* I'd been sure Royce Allen was involved. He'd heard me talking about the car. He hated Lee. He could have easily written that message on my mirror while I was having coffee with Mr. Huffman.

At least Chief McTavish saved me from wasting time and money sending Hal to verify Royce Allen's alibi. Assuming my phone held up long enough, I'd send him a text as soon as I left, telling him not to continue looking into Royce.

My idea didn't hinge on Royce being the one who killed Lee, though. "I wasn't saying Royce Allen was necessarily the one who killed Lee Mills." At least I wasn't saying that anymore, but McTavish didn't need to know I'd been thinking Royce lied about his alibi. "All I was saying was he gave me the idea. He said maybe someone meant to steal Lee's car, and Lee resisted. If they did that, they might still have sold the car whole, otherwise the murder would have been for nothing."

McTavish lowered his arms and straightened slightly in his chair, a dead giveaway that he was coming around to my point of view even if he didn't want to admit it.

"That would have been a risky move. Your husband thinks the victim died from a blow to the temple. There could have been blood involved."

Another point for McTavish. Not that this was a game where we were on opposite sides. In the end, we actually both wanted the same thing. McTavish and I often disagreed on who'd committed a crime, but we both wanted to see the right person—rather than the convenient person—charged with the crime.

So I'd follow his line of reasoning. "If the killer sold the car to a person rather than for parts, that likely would have come to light by now. You'd have uncovered someone who stole and sold cars when you were investigating Chief Wilson's cover-ups. Or someone would have talked about buying a stolen car or the police somewhere would have noticed the car when the search was on for Lee Mills when everyone thought he was missing."

My words came out a bit rambling, but McTavish nodded through it.

And yet, someone was scared enough about me finding the car to try to get me to stop. It had to still be out there somewhere. "Did the reports the officers made when they first investigated mention anyone in the area who might have seen something? The officers might have originally asked them about people or about a single car, thinking Lee would have been driving off alone. They might not have thought to ask about two vehicles together." Whoever attacked Lee likely hadn't walked there on foot. They would have needed a partner who drove their car away after.

"They didn't find anyone who was in the area at the time to question, about cars or otherwise," McTavish said.

I wanted to stomp my foot, but McTavish would see that as

childish. Wait—Mr. Huffman said something about driving around in case kids decided to make car tunnels through his crops for fun. He probably thought he hadn't seen anything since he didn't see what he was looking for. That didn't mean he might not have spotted Lee's vehicle being driven away by the killer without even realizing what he'd seen.

I filled Chief McTavish in on what Mr. Huffman said.

"I'll look into it."

McTavish stood up, signaling that he was done discussing the situation with me. I'd only earned this much leeway because someone threatened me.

I rose as slowly as possible, but I couldn't think of anything to say to keep the discussion open. As soon as his office door closed behind me, we'd be back to *I can't tell you anything about an open investigation.*

"You probably hear this from everyone." Chief McTavish opened the door for me. "And you'll probably ignore me the way you do them, but be careful. I don't want to have to be the one to tell your husband that you were shot at again or fished out of the lake because someone ran the car you were in off the road."

I couldn't rank all the near-death situations I'd experienced in order of awfulness. If I had, that one would have been near the top because I wasn't the only one who almost drown. We'd been sitting in a car when our attacker nudged it over a bluff and into the lake. The woman I was with was knocked unconscious. The car sank almost immediately.

I froze. "The car I was in sank."

McTavish made a small shooing motion with his hand like he wanted to get on with his day and he couldn't do that until I left. "And you were lucky to make it out alive. Whoever sent that note was right, in a way. Your luck will run out eventually."

I let the jab pass. I was careful. I tried to be, at least. "No, I mean if I wanted to get rid of a car and make sure no one found it, I'd push it into the lake."

11

*T*om McClanahan's hello on the phone the next day sent nervous flutters up from my belly and into my throat, where they tried to choke me. It wasn't the hello of a person who had good news that the deal was done, and that we needed to have our bank send Mr. Huffman's lawyer the money.

It was the hello of a man who thought he might be fired. Or sued.

I was used to being around other criminal defense attorneys. The tone in his voice wasn't one I was used to hearing from another lawyer.

I sat on the floor between Toby and Velma, where they'd dropped after our long walk. Toby's snoring barely hiccupped at my presence, but Velma moved her head into my lap. I stroked her favorite spot behind her ears. I might need their comfort if whatever Tom had to say was half as bad as it sounded.

At least I could hear him clearly. Mark had the morning off, so we'd gone to replace my phone as soon as we'd woken up. I'd set up my fingerprint ID right away because I hated having to type in my passcode, and Mark helped me transfer everything from my old phone to my new one. It was surprisingly easy to get all my favorite apps switched over. Mark had teased me that we needed to do it right away since one of the apps was Phone Finder, and it was likely the first thing I'd do with a new phone was lose it. Considering I'd wrecked my new car shortly after buying it, I didn't want to tempt fate by not getting Phone Finder back onto my phone immediately.

"I don't know how to tell you this," Tom said. I could imagine him pushing his wire-rimmed glasses higher up on his nose. "I called Mr. Huffman's lawyer yesterday after you were in to sign the papers, but their office was already closed. I put the signed documents into my filing cabinet and locked it. When I came back this morning, they were gone."

Papers didn't spontaneously combust. They also didn't sprout legs and walk away.

Mr. Huffman hadn't been right about me not being invested in his deal, but he might have been partly right. Someone didn't want this sale to happen.

Only two people came to mind—whoever the other buyer was and Ashley. Actually, Ashley had to have been involved either way. The other buyer wouldn't have been able to break into McClanahan & Associates without leaving some sign of forced entry. Tom hadn't mentioned signs of a break-in.

Maybe the other buyer paid her to continue delaying our paperwork until they could convince Mr. Huffman to take their offer instead. On Ashley's side, I could see her accepting money to delay us. All the plastic surgery she'd had must cost more than she could easily cover on her salary, even if she were a legal assistant rather than a secretary. I hadn't pushed to find out her official designations. I hadn't cared before.

I didn't want to believe she hated me enough to do this out of spite alone. Not booking appointments and being snotty was one thing. This was a whole other level. All I'd ever done to her was marry Mark, and that wasn't even done directly to her. She and Mark had never even dated. It wasn't my fault her feelings for him had never been reciprocated.

"I have Ashley searching the filing cabinets," Tom was saying as if I'd missed a whole apology speech while I was lost in my thoughts. "I was tired last night. It's possible I misfiled it."

His sentence ended, but in that drawn-out way that said more was coming.

"I went to the computer to print off our standard template and start filling it in again because I know you both want this deal done. It wasn't there."

I leaned forward and rested my head on top of Velma's. Her warm doggy smell helped ease the tension in my body.

Whoever was behind this had made certain we wouldn't be signing the files again today.

I straightened up. "You need to call the police." I wasn't comfortable telling Tom my suspicions about Ashley. I had no real proof, and my judgment could be clouded by my own negative feelings toward her. If I were wrong, I'd be planting doubt and jeopardizing her job. The only way around that was to make sure someone I knew investigated the case so I could call them before they even got there to fill them in. "Ask for Sergeant Erik Higgins or Officer Elise Scott."

And on the up side, I'd have something non-case-related to talk to Mark about tonight. I was tired of starting sentences only to realize I couldn't finish them.

12

"I'm using up a lot of favors on you," Chief McTavish said over the phone.

I waved at Russ to go on ahead of me and continue checking on our saplings. I didn't want to risk walking into a dead zone and losing Chief McTavish if he was calling about the Lee Mills case. Even a new phone couldn't fix Fair Haven dead zones.

Russ didn't really need me to check the trees. It was more me trying to stay involved in Sugarwood business. With the signed paperwork still missing and the electronic copies deleted, we were coming out every other day to check the trees. Some of them looked better than others. Russ figured we were days away from losing a quarter of them.

"I only remember one favor so far," I said. While Mark and I were on our honeymoon, I'd accidentally ended up in the middle of a missing person's case, and McTavish had contacted a friend at the FBI on my behalf.

"Then this makes two. We weren't going to be given the

budget to search the lake for Mills' missing car. Even I have people above me, and they thought it was too much of a long shot for such an old case."

In my opinion, the age of a case shouldn't matter. A murderer was no less a murderer whether it happened ten days or ten years ago. Cold cases were notoriously harder to close, though, and some officials felt they shouldn't be given much of a budget at all. Mark's younger brother Bobby was struggling with that very problem right now. He'd recently transferred from homicide to a special cold case team, and their budget seemed smaller than any other departments'.

Given that knowledge, I probably shouldn't aggravate Chief McTavish. "So you called in a favor and got permission to drag the lake once the ice breaks?"

Spring was a long time to wait for answers, especially for Daphne, who would have the possibility of arrest looming over her until this was resolved. Still, spring was better than never if Daphne was arrested because they didn't have evidence that pointed elsewhere.

McTavish sighed. "Why don't you let me tell the story, Nicole?"

I pressed my mitted hand over my mouth to stop a laugh from sneaking out. Since we'd met, Chief McTavish had tried to avoid using my first name. Now he couldn't get around it. Calling me Cavanaugh would be too confusing since Mark also worked for the county. Calling me Fitzhenry-Dawes—or just Dawes, since he seemed to find the whole thing too much of a mouthful—would have meant acknowledging he was giving information to the lawyer of a person of interest in an open case.

"Go ahead." I wasn't entirely successful in keeping the laughter out of my voice.

"I know someone who works for the Environmental Protection Agency, and they have satellite imagery of the lake from when they did their human pollution study a few years ago. They'd identified all large foreign bodies."

That would include shipwrecks, but it would also include cars. "They know where to find Lee Mills' car?"

McTavish didn't sigh again, but I could almost hear him thinking it. "You couldn't help yourself." His voice carried a hint of a smile. "We found the car, and because I could show exactly where it was, I got permission to haul it out immediately."

I indulged in a mini happy dance. Anyone watching would have thought I was trying to stay warm.

"As soon as it's back at the impound garage, we'll tear it apart. If you're right, the car will point us in a direction away from your client."

I TUGGED ON THE TRUNK OF THE DEAD SAPLING WHILE RUSS GAVE one final heave. The tree made it over the edge of the tailgate.

We'd knocked as much dirt off what Russ called the rootball as we could, but the tree was still heavy enough that my shoulders ached like I'd tried to do a hundred push-ups.

My phone buzzed in my pocket.

"Go ahead and get it," Russ said, his breath coming out in white puffs. "I need a rest anyway. Might be time to hire some young muscle on a full-time basis."

I nodded my agreement and pulled out my phone. Every time it'd rung in the past two days since McTavish's call about the car, I'd been hoping it was him calling back with more news. It was a futile wish. McTavish wasn't going to share anything more about the case with me. The update on the car had been a courtesy since I helped him find it.

"This is Nikki," I said into my phone.

"It's Tom McClanahan. I got all the paperwork redone and printed off for you. I was thinking the best way to handle this would be if you, Russ, and Mr. Huffman came in and all signed at once. I have an hour open now if that works for you. It shouldn't take much longer than that for us to finally have this deal done."

I filled Russ in, and he waved his hand in a go-ahead motion. He was probably glad we had an excuse for not loading the other two dead trees today.

"We'll be there," I told Tom. "Did the police find anything that could point to who did this?"

"Unfortunately not. They say there weren't any signs of forced entry, and they asked Ashley and me a lot of questions about who could have had access to our keys. They're not optimistic."

Not publicly, anyway. Elise had hinted to me afterward that she'd be finding out the name of Mr. Huffman's other buyer and asking Ashley's phone company for her records. Because phone records were about a person but not owned by a person, the police could get them without a warrant. If something fishy showed up on the phone records, it would enable Elise to get a warrant for Ashley's bank accounts to check for strange deposits.

Either way, the best thing we could do was get the papers signed and then not take our eyes off of them until they were in the hands of Mr. Huffman and his lawyer.

I climbed into the cab of Russ' truck, and my phone dinged with a text this time.

I need you at Daphne's house immediately, Grady wrote.

With the car now found, there was nothing that could be so urgent it couldn't wait until later this afternoon.

In the middle of something, I wrote back. *I can come around 4pm.*

The three dots that indicated Grady was writing a reply rolled on the screen. They stayed there long enough that I wasn't sure if he planned to write anything more or if he'd started and abandoned the text. I hated how the dots sometimes stayed even when it became clear the other person wasn't going to send whatever they'd written.

The sound of a text arriving hit my ears before my eyes could focus on the words.

They found a credit card belonging to Case Hammond in Lee Mills' car.

The hand holding my phone felt disconnected from the rest of my body. There was only one reason for Case's credit card to be in that car—he'd been in the car and it fell out of his pocket. He hadn't noticed it.

And there was only one reason I could think of that Case Hammond would have been in Lee's car—he'd killed Lee and driven his car to the spot where he pushed it into the lake.

13

*M*y text telling Grady that this was actually good news in a way because they wouldn't be looking at Daphne anymore for Lee's murder was answered with a curt *Get here ASAP.*

I signed all my papers first and arranged for Mr. Huffman to give Russ a ride back to Sugarwood. I drove Russ' truck, dead sapling and all, to Daphne's home.

They must have been watching for me because Grady opened the door as soon as I pulled into the driveway. He still wore his police uniform.

A tickle formed at the back of my throat. Something wasn't right.

I could understand Grady being upset. Someone he thought was his friend hid this from him all this time, even when the police were looking at Daphne. Grady might think Case wouldn't have admitted the truth even if Daphne had been convicted.

But Grady was here still in his uniform. He'd either come with the news directly after his shift ended or he'd left during his shift. To bring news that he shouldn't have shared. As Chief McTavish loved to tell me, this was an open investigation, and the police didn't share information involving an open investigation with civilians.

Grady's gaze hopped from my purple knee-high snow boots to my Uncle Stan's oversized winter jacket that I wore when working at Sugarwood to my ear muffs. The smirk that crossed his face made me want to slam the door and go back home.

No, I don't look professional, you jerk, I wanted to say. *You demanded I come right away.*

It almost erased all the goodwill he'd earned as I'd learned more about his childhood.

I pushed past him and into the warm house. "What's going on that couldn't wait?"

Daphne stood inside the door, near the bottom of the stairs. Neither she nor Grady shushed me. Gina must be at school.

"I already told you what's going on," Grady said.

Dear Lord, give me patience, I prayed. I didn't need to be here if there was nothing else to say. I could have stayed and made sure we didn't hit another snag with the farm purchase.

Grady hooked his thumbs along his belt. "You weren't supposed to get Case arrested in place of Daphne. That wasn't the deal."

I slowly pulled off my work gloves and tucked them into my coat pockets. The *deal* was that I'd defend Daphne. Nowhere in any of our conversations had he said I should defend Daphne as long as it didn't end up pointing the finger of blame at anyone on his mental list of other people. Besides, it wasn't like I'd planted Case's credit card in Lee Mills' car. I hadn't been anywhere around the car since they pulled it out of the lake. Chief McTavish made sure of that.

Case must have been the one who left the threatening note on my car mirror, too. I hadn't thought about him when I'd talked to Chief McTavish about people who knew I was searching for Lee Mills' car, but Case had been here when I asked Daphne about it.

This crime seemed solved. All that was left for me to do was to help them accept it.

I angled my body toward Grady first, facing him straight-on, professional to professional. "I know it can be hard to find out that someone you trusted lied to you—believe me, I do—but that credit card is pretty condemning evidence, especially if the police check the records and find out the last time it was used was the day of Lee's murder." I shifted a little so that I could make eye contact with Daphne. "I think he even left a threatening message for me after I was here last time. He knew I planned to look for Lee's car. He didn't want anyone finding it because he knew what they'd find in it."

"Case didn't kill Lee." Daphne's voice had the thick quality of someone who'd been crying and couldn't clear their head. "And we left that note for you together. Or, at least, I told him what to write."

All along I'd had a feeling Daphne hadn't told me the whole truth. Now I was sure. My parents would drop a client who lied to them like this. They'd certainly drop any client who threatened them. Normally I would, too, but that danged favor hung over my head like my own personal storm cloud. "Why wouldn't you have just told me what was going on? I took the message on my mirror to the police because I thought the car would help clear you."

Daphne hung her head.

Grady pointed to the coat rack. "Finish taking off your stuff. I told her she has to explain it all to you."

I left my coat and boots behind and followed them back to a living room I was becoming all too familiar with.

This time I took the armchair before anyone else could. Based on the way the living room was laid out, it felt like the position of authority, and I'd let my sense of obligation to Grady rule this whole situation for far too long. "I need to know it all this time, or I'm done." I met Grady's gaze. "Favor or no favor."

The look on his face said he wished pirates and walking the plank were still a thing because he'd love to see me fed to the sharks. But he kept his mouth shut. It seemed like his love for his sister was kryptonite to his pride.

Daphne grabbed two tissues from a box beside the couch. "I told you most of the truth. Lee and I hooked up that night, and I admitted to him that I was pregnant. He didn't want me to keep the baby, we argued, and I left." She swallowed and dabbed the tissues under her nose. "What I didn't tell you was that I went back."

Little black dots swam in my vision. All I could do was pray she wasn't about to tell me she'd gone back and cracked Lee in the temple. Or that she'd told Case what happened and he went back and killed Lee for her. I'd made a promise, but I didn't want to defend someone who was guilty, and I'd have to try to convince her to take a plea bargain. Conspiracy to commit murder carried the same penalty as being the one to pull the trigger. Or in this case, make the killing blow.

Daphne sniffled. "I got partway to town and decided I didn't want my baby to grow up without a dad the way I had. I shouldn't have stormed off. I should have stayed and talked it through with him. I was sure he'd see it my way if I tried hard enough."

A bitter edge had entered her voice. In hindsight, she probably knew better, but she'd been young and scared and desperate.

"Go on," I said softly. "It's better if you tell me everything."

Daphne nodded. "I should have told you from the start, but I hadn't even told Grady. Not until today. Case and I agreed we'd never tell anyone."

A chill swept over me like I'd stepped out into a sub-zero night without a coat on. No sentence that included *we agreed never to tell anyone* could possibly lead to something good.

Beyond that, we were going to have a much bigger problem if they had killed Lee. She'd already told Grady whatever she was about to tell me. He could be forced to testify against her.

"You let her tell you?" I said. I couldn't keep the disbelief out of my voice. Or the disappointment.

Grady's normally plank-straight posture hunched. "I didn't know what she was going to say until it was too late. I came over because I wanted her to hear the news about Case from me."

Daphne's gaze bounced between us. "Why is that bad?"

"We have to make sure no one else knows that I know,

okay?" Grady moved around the couch and sat next to her, showing solidarity. "Tell her the rest."

Grady seemed to have the same problem with my first name as Chief McTavish, but for different reasons. Using my first name would make us seem like friends. Using my last name gave me a level of respect he wasn't willing to dole out.

Daphne pulled her legs up onto the couch to sit cross-legged, the way she had the first night we met. "By the time I walked back..." Her hands shook. She glanced back at Grady. "Why doesn't it get easier to tell?"

She took his hand. I had to give him big brother points for the fact that she'd grabbed his hand with the hand that she had the tissues in and he didn't even flinch.

Daphne's knuckles turned white. "Lee was dead by the time I got back. There's was blood all over his face. His clothes. I panicked. I knew if I called the police, they'd blame me. My DNA was all over his car. We'd had a public fight. I was carrying his baby. And I had no money to hire a real lawyer."

The side of me that still doubted my abilities as a lawyer tried to tell me this was game over. That either she or Case or both of them were going to prison for Lee's murder.

But the part of me that didn't know how to quit whispered that this was a partial win. I now knew a very precise time of death. I held on to that part.

I still hadn't heard the whole story, but I had a feeling I knew where this was headed now. "So you called Case?"

"Grady was away. Case was the only other person I trusted. He worked as a dispatcher. I knew he'd know what to do."

He should have known to call the police. Then again, I'd

been raised by two successful criminal defense attorneys. I'd never had to be afraid I wouldn't have someone to stick up for me. My parents might not have been the most emotionally supportive people, but they'd proven that, when I really needed them, they would be there.

Daphne pulled out more tissues with her free hand. It looked like she didn't plan to continue, like she wanted me to fill in the gaps about what happened next.

"I'm sorry," I said, "but I have to hear it all."

"We buried Lee in the field, and then I drove Case's car while he drove Lee's. Case thought it would be better that way. If anyone recognized Lee's car and saw a man driving it, they'd assume it was Lee. We pushed the car off a bluff and into the lake to make it look like Lee left town."

That was improper disposal of a body at the very least. I wasn't sure exactly what it would be for dumping a car into the lake, but destruction of evidence for certain. This wasn't good. Even though they hadn't killed Lee, they were looking at fines and jail time. Case would lose his job.

"What do we do now?" Daphne's voice had a desperate edge to it that I hadn't heard before, even when she was being questioned by the police. "How do we fix this?"

I didn't know if we could fix this. They were guilty, just not of murder.

And I wasn't as sure as Daphne was that Case hadn't killed Lee to protect her. I had a suspicion he loved her now, and he'd loved her then.

Until I could sort out exactly what had happened, we needed to keep this from getting any worse. "First, I need to text Case and tell him to exercise his right to remain silent. I can represent him, but you both need to sign a waiver. It's a conflict of interest to represent you both otherwise. And if you two have any sort of feelings for each other, I'd consider a quick wedding. If you're married, they can't force you to testify against each other."

he look Chief McTavish gave me when Case and I walked out of the station was one that said he'd never be doing me a favor again. I'd basically promised him that Lee Mills' car would solve this case for him, and then once he found evidence, I'd had to stonewall him.

I hadn't allowed Case to say anything, and I'd provided a list of all the other ways Case's credit card could have gotten into Lee's car that night. Case could have dropped it there some other time. Lee could have stolen it—he did have a record of theft. Whoever really killed Lee could have stolen it and planted it there to frame Case.

What I wasn't able to prevent was Case being put on administrative suspension pending further investigation. That investigation would eventually turn up when Case's credit card was last active, and half my excuses for how it got there would be wiped away.

My parents would have called the interview a win. In fact, if I called them and told them about what I'd done, I knew they'd be proud of me. Their praise was so hard to earn that I almost made the call.

Until I remembered the way I felt sitting across from Chief McTavish and knowing he felt I tricked him. It left me feeling like I had a coating of slime on my skin that wouldn't wash off.

Instead, as soon as Case and I parted ways, I called Mark. "I really need takeout tonight."

"I'm on my way home. I'll swing by A Salt & Battery and meet you there."

I tried to pretend there hadn't been a touch of relief in his voice. Tonight had been my night to cook again, and considering I only knew how to cook three dishes, he'd probably been dreading that we were going to be eating soggy spaghetti and meatballs again.

By the time I got home, Mark had already taken the dogs out for a quick walk and fed them. For all the changes that required some getting used to—like we went through groceries twice as fast and had to do laundry twice as often—the good definitely outweighed the challenges. It was nice to come home and not have to worry about the dogs or about dinner some nights.

I updated Mark on getting the documents signed, and then silence fell again. I glanced up from my fish and chips. Mark was watching me.

He reached a hand out toward me. I placed my palm in his.

"I think I figured it out," he said. "Why you're so quiet and down tonight."

He couldn't mean the weird situation with the farm sale. We actually had positive progress in that direction.

"At first I thought I'd done something you were angry about." He stroked the back of my hand with his thumb. "But you're not the kind of person to give the silent treatment when you're angry."

He knew me well enough to know I rarely held anything in. I was more likely to blurt than I was to stew. I was going to get an ulcer if I had to keep going the way I was not telling him about my cases. "I'm not angry. It's—"

"Your requirement for client confidentiality." He flashed me a smile with full dimples. "I figured it out when you told me about the trees and then that you only stayed long enough to sign your spaces on the paperwork. Given all that's going on, you wouldn't have left unless something more important pulled you away."

If Mark had been paunchy and bald with acne but still had the same mind, I would have married him. The fact that he was handsome was an added bonus. "In the past, I was either working with the police so we could talk openly or you weren't involved in the case, and I got permission from my client to share details. This time, we're working on opposite sides in a way we haven't been before. I didn't know how to handle it."

It felt like I should have known how to handle this, but I'd grown up with parents who worked together. They'd never had to keep things from each other in the name of confidentiality.

Mark squeezed my hand. "We all go through it at some point. It's harder when you're married."

He'd gone through this before with Laura. If I hadn't had so many issues jumbled up in my mind, I probably would have remembered that sooner. He knew what it was like to have to find the balance with your spouse of sharing an important part of your life without violating your professional responsibilities. "So how do I find the line?"

He let my hand go and ate another bite. Mark hated it when food got cold. It was one of his endearing quirks. I often took cold pasta from the fridge for a snack. My cooking was actually better the next day.

"I ask myself if what I want to tell you is public knowledge. I can tell you I went to the site of an accident. I can tell you the police don't think it was an accident. I can't tell you the identity of the victims until the police release the names, and I can't tell you anything they're going to hold back from the press."

The circumstances would be a bit trickier for me. Sometimes clients told me things other people knew that weren't exactly common knowledge. I'd have to make my best guess and trust that my heart and instincts would work together.

"I'm representing Case Hammond along with Daphne Scherwin for the murder of Lee Mills," I blurted.

Mark's fork wobbled. "I'd heard a rumor that Case was on suspension. I thought it was just a rumor. He's a good guy."

Case had a propensity to play rescuer more than he should, even down to trying to protect Daphne from me when I was her lawyer. I could see his grumpiness with me and avoidance of my calls for what they were now—he didn't want me to find out that he and Daphne had dumped Lee's body.

But when I weighed all the evidence, I had to think maybe Mark was right. Case Hammond was a decent guy.

"The chief wouldn't have suspended Case unless he had strong evidence against him," Mark said. "Are you sure about this case? We made Grady a deal, but you don't have to do anything you're not comfortable with."

I wasn't comfortable with this case for so many reasons, but not for the reason Mark assumed. He had to mean that I didn't have to work this case if it meant violating my principles and defending a guilty person.

I finished my last bite of fish, letting the flakiness practically melt in my mouth. I wanted to explain to Mark why I felt committed to this case, but this was my first test. I couldn't tell him what they'd done that night and that they claimed they hadn't killed Lee.

I could tell him what I knew about them as people. "I want to. It's like you said, Case Hammond is a good guy. And Daphne is a single mom with a sick kid."

Mark went to the cupboard and brought back a plate covered with aluminum foil. "Compliments of Nancy." He pulled back the foil to reveal cookies filled with cream. From the color, maple syrup was likely involved in the recipe. "What's wrong with Daphne's daughter?"

The fact that Grady hadn't talked about Gina's illness at work probably shouldn't have surprised me. He didn't seem embarrassed by her or Daphne, but bringing his personal life to work would have tarnished the perfect-cop image he seemed to want to maintain.

I bit into a cookie. Why didn't I have this skill? Baking made everyone happy. Instead I got the skill that came with death threats and people who lied. Mark's mom would say it was because God gifted everyone according to the special purpose He had for them. Someone had to defend the innocent and chase the truth. Besides, based on my most recent conversation with my friend Isabel, being a baker wasn't any guarantee of safety. She'd already gotten herself embroiled in a murder investigation since leaving Fair Haven.

"Nikki? You're not in a sugar coma already, are you?"

I couldn't help but smile. It faded as fast as it came thinking about Gina and how she was in danger of losing the people who took care of her. Could Grady care for her on his own if both Daphne and Case ended up in prison? "Sickle cell anemia. Daphne's only real family support is Grady. Her daughter's dad is dead, and his parents cut them off when they found out Gina was sick. They said it was a genetic disorder, and it didn't run in their family so she couldn't be their granddaughter."

Mark finished chewing and reached for another cookie. "They're right."

I shook my head. "It runs in Daphne's family. Gina got it from her side."

Mark laid his half-eaten cookie down. "Not if she has sickle cell anemia. It's inherited in an autosomal recessive pattern. Both parents have to carry the gene for the child to have it. If only one parent passes on the gene, then the child would only be a carrier."

Biology had never been my thing in high school. I was too squeamish to ever want to know what happened inside of any body, including my own. *Autosomal recessive* meant nothing to me, but Mark's explanation did.

Lee Mills couldn't be Gina's father.

But I knew someone who could, and the whole lying group of them was about to lose me as a lawyer unless they could give me a really good reason to stay. They couldn't say I hadn't warned them.

15

I texted Daphne and told her I'd be there in ten minutes—no arguments—and that I wanted to talk to her alone.

She was the one I was most likely able to break. In part because she was a woman and I was a woman, but also because her first priority was Gina. If she lost me and had to go with a public defender, her chances of staying out of prison went down dramatically. She was lucky I wasn't my parents.

Daphne had the front step light on when I pulled up. Inside, I stripped off my coat and shoes and headed straight for her living room without being invited. Daphne wore pink sweat pants, a white t-shirt, and a big, fuzzy cardigan, like she'd been ready for bed.

She stood back a bit, her lips tight. "Are the police coming to arrest me?"

The simple ask aimed a high-powered fire extinguisher at

the anger flames I'd been fanning since I figured it out. Maybe she needed to be a little scared first to make her finally be honest with me, but seeing someone that frightened didn't make me feel good. It made me want to run right at whatever was frightening them and take it out. In this case, I'd be taking out myself.

I ran my fingers through my hair. "Please sit. The police aren't coming. At least not right now. But you've lied to me again, and this was the last strike."

Her eyebrows pulled down in the middle, and she sank to the edge of the couch. "I don't know what you mean. I've told you everything now."

If I didn't know better, I would have said she was telling the truth. "Lee wasn't Gina's father. Case is. Sickle cell anemia has to be inherited from both parents. You can't get it from only one."

Daphne shook her head, but then her mouth drooped open. "It was only one time."

Aaand now I was a bit angry at myself. "You didn't know."

She shook her head again like she couldn't help herself. "I thought she was Lee's. Lee and I were sleeping together regularly, and Case and I...like I said, it was just once."

I was pretty sure "just once" was all it ever took, but I could see how she would have assumed the baby was Lee's. "If I figured this out, the police won't be far behind. It could look like Case killed Lee because you wouldn't leave him."

"I don't think so." She wrapped her sweater tighter around her, like she needed the comfort. "Maybe. It happened because I found out that Lee had cheated on me again, and I needed someone to talk to. Grady was at work, so I went to Case. He said I shouldn't be with someone who didn't respect me enough to be faithful to me. I told him I couldn't break up with Lee. Who else would want me?" Her lips picked up the tiniest bit at the corners. "Case said he would. When he said it, I figured out I'd been in love with him for years."

She didn't need to open the closed door. I could imagine where things went from there.

Daphne scrubbed a hand across her eyes. "Case worked nights for the next few weeks. We didn't get a chance to talk about what had happened and what it meant for us. By the time we did, I'd found out I was pregnant, and I thought it was Lee's. I felt like I had to get back together with him. He promised he wouldn't cheat again."

I had a pretty good guess what happened next. "But he did."

"He did. I hadn't gotten up the courage yet to tell him about the baby." Daphne sucked her hands into her sleeves. "We had that big fight in front of Hops that everyone saw. He called me afterward and told me that the girl I heard about was before we got back together. So I took him back. I thought I had to. I was having his baby. If I hadn't gone back to him, I wouldn't have been anywhere near where he was killed that night."

She could see her mistakes now in hindsight, but she shouldn't blame herself for not seeing them then.

Still, it left us with a huge problem. The police were going to see motive in the fact that Case and Daphne slept together and Case was the actual father of her child.

I moved from the chair to the couch. "Are you one hundred percent sure that Case didn't kill Lee to protect you?"

She looked down at her knees and then back up to my face.

"You should have seen his face that night. He was scared. He made me promise that I hadn't killed Lee."

"Then we need to work together to figure out who might have wanted Lee dead. Because unless I find the real killer, I think Case is going to prison for this."

16

I stayed with Daphne for another two hours. She walked me through that night again in detail. None of my questions yielded anything new or useful.

We moved on to the names of the women Lee cheated with. The only good possibility I could come up with was that one of them—or an angry dad, brother, or boyfriend—had done something to Lee. I didn't recognize any of the names, which meant I'd need Hal to track down their current addresses and phone numbers for me.

I told her to include anyone she knew or suspected Lee cheated with. She only knew of three for sure, but the suspected list added five more names.

Once I left, I sat in my car for a minute, waiting for it to warm up, and texted the list to Hal, despite the late hour.

A response pinged in before I could put my car into drive. *Received. Might not be able to get to them until Monday.*

It was only Thursday night. Finding addresses and current phone numbers for the people on my list shouldn't have been that much of a challenge for Hal. I'd had him dig up much more difficult information.

Another text zipped into my phone.

Anderson has me digging up information that he thinks could make a case. He needs it by Monday. I'll be working all weekend as is.

It might be time for Hal to hire more staff. We weren't even his only clients. But in this situation, Anderson's task had to take precedence. Case hadn't been arrested yet. My curiosity might take a hit from waiting to track down Lee Mills' romantic conquests, but my clients wouldn't.

Unfortunately, it meant I couldn't pawn off going to McClanahan & Associates tomorrow on Russ using the excuse that I was too busy. Until Hal got me information on my list of names, my investigation was at a standstill.

THE NEXT MORNING, I SAT IN MY CAR OUTSIDE McCLANAHAN & Associates for five minutes before I convinced myself to turn off the engine. Turning it off gave me a timeline. I'd soon get cold and have to go in.

Suspecting what I did about Ashley being behind all the delays in the purchase of our property—not to mention the trees that died as a consequence—made me wish I could pull an ostrich rather than facing her.

I shouldn't drag my feet. Our payment had been accepted by Mr. Huffman's bank, and all available Sugarwood staff were out in the field, trying to get our surviving saplings into the ground. I'd teased Mark when I'd kissed him goodbye that it was awfully convenient he had a conference to attend this weekend in Ohio.

With a day of hard work ahead, I'd only broken away from the tree planting to pay our bill. Between Russ and me, I was the expendable one when it came to planting the trees. I didn't have nearly the experience Russ had. It made sense for me to go.

That, and Elise and I had agreed that I should mention to Tom that I felt Ashley had caused unnecessary delays and that made me concerned she might be behind my paperwork disappearing. Elise couldn't say anything officially yet. We thought Tom should know in the meantime so he could keep a closer watch on her until she'd either been cleared or Elise found solid evidence.

The heat had drained out of my car, and cold nipped at the exposed skin on my face.

Maybe this was so difficult because I'd never had to fire anyone. Approaching Tom with this information felt like signing Ashley's pink slip. If she turned out to be innocent, I'd have placed unfounded doubt about her in his mind. Then again, I knew for a fact that she'd maliciously failed to schedule my appointments with him in the past. Having Tom observe her behavior more closely for a short period of time wouldn't hurt. It might even make doing future business with them more pleasant if she turned out to be innocent.

I placed a hand on the door handle, and my phone rang.

Elise's name and a picture of her with her kids flashed on the screen.

Perhaps she had the evidence she needed, and I wouldn't have to be the one to talk to Tom after all.

"I got the phone number of the other buyer from Mr. Huffman," Elise said, "and it doesn't match any incoming or outgoing calls from Ashley's phone records."

Granted, I didn't like Ashley, but even objectively, the evidence seemed to point to her. Elise had suspected her, too.

"You checked both her home phone and cell phone?"

Elise made an *mmhmm* noise. "She only has a cell phone, and I requested them for a full month before you even started negotiating with Mr. Huffman."

Ashley could have a burner phone, but that implied a certain amount of savvy and forethought for covering her tracks that the rest of this situation didn't show. A woman who went to the trouble of buying a burner phone would have also left obvious signs of a break-in so that the police wouldn't suspect it was an inside job.

Besides, if she had bought a burner phone, we'd have no way of knowing or tracking it.

"What about other numbers?" I asked. "For the buyer. If they're a big corporation the way it sounded, they might have multiple phone numbers."

"I checked that, too." Elise sounded like she would have patted herself on the back had her arms been long enough. "None of the numbers associated with them either called or were called by Ashley."

I tapped my fingers on the armrest. That meant that Ashley

probably wasn't involved in what had happened. Maybe it was all my imagination. Maybe there was no big conspiracy.

Except that someone had deleted files from their computer system. The odds of that happening accidentally at the very wrong time were astronomically small.

Now I didn't know how to proceed. "Do I still talk to Tom McClanahan as planned?"

"You can't." All self-congratulation was gone from Elise's voice. "If it wasn't Ashley, then Tom is most likely our mole."

At any other time, Elise using the word *mole*, like we were in a spy movie, would have made me crack up.

But my heart just felt heavy this time. Tom wasn't a defense attorney like I was, but we were both lawyers. Why would he do something like this? He could be disbarred. Depending on how hard the Fair Haven police decided they wanted to be, he could face fines or even jail time if they considered it a form of corporate espionage.

Lawyers did illegal things all the time, but I couldn't see it in this case. Reading people was my gift. Even though I hadn't felt I needed to read Tom, I should have noticed something off in the many conversations we had about this purchase.

It couldn't be him. Someone must have broken into their offices using a stolen key. That would have been a great cover for the real thief since all eyes would focus on Tom or Ashley.

My brain clicked in to the fact that Elise was still talking.

"I'm trying to get a hold of Tom's phone records. We'll see if they give us any better answers."

I nodded and then remembered she couldn't see me. "Let me know what you find out."

In the meantime, I'd pay my bill like nothing was wrong. I couldn't let either of them see that I suspected anything. If I tipped Tom off and he turned out to be behind this, he'd have time to destroy any evidence—of this and any other shady dealing he'd helped with in the past.

17

J'd once thought that snowshoeing was of the devil based on how it made my body feel like I'd been in a car wreck. Planting trees was worse.

A long, hot soak in the tub didn't even help. Then again, neither did the fact that Mark still hadn't called by the time I got out and dressed. He'd promised to call once he arrived and settled in, and that would have been a couple hours ago.

Maybe I should make sure my ringer was turned on. Sometimes when I dropped my phone into my purse, the sound button flicked to the off position.

If it was on, I'd give him ten more minutes and then I'd call him. Considering that worrying about me was part of his regular routine, he couldn't even tease me about jumping the gun and worrying enough about him to call.

Besides, this would be our first night apart since we got married. I already didn't like it. I should have taken Russ up on his offer to babysit the dogs so I could follow Mark there. We only had about a dozen trees left to plant, and Russ had called in some of our seasonal workers to help, so he didn't need me around tomorrow.

I rifled absentmindedly through my purse for my phone. Actually, there wasn't anything here that needed me for the weekend. Ohio wasn't that far. I could pack up and surprise Mark. It would have been better if we'd driven together, but on the way home, we could drive "together" via Bluetooth phone call. I'd love to curl up and read a new mystery while he was in sessions. Maybe I'd even be able to sneak in and learn something new about forensic medicine that could help in a future case.

I pulled open the lips of my purse in earnest. Where was my phone?

I moved over to the counter and dumped everything out.

No phone.

So I must have left it in a coat pocket. I searched the pockets of my dress coat, my regular coat, and Uncle Stan's old coat that I still liked to wear sometimes when working around Sugarwood.

No phone.

Oh no. When we were planting the last of the trees, Russ saw me put it in my pocket and he warned me about it getting crushed. I'd taken it out and set it on that big fallen tree on the edge of the bush. I must not have picked it back up.

Not only would Mark be frantic if he'd been trying to reach me, but I certainly couldn't drive to Ohio without a phone. Not with my navigational skills—or lack thereof.

I grabbed a flashlight from the shelf where we kept it in case of a power outage. I had to go get my phone.

THE TEMPERATURE HAD DROPPED AGAIN, LOW ENOUGH THAT IT felt like my lungs might freeze. I wrapped a scarf around my head and face so only my eyes peered out. When I first saw Mandy do it in preparation for a walk with the dogs, I'd told her she looked like a pink bandit. By the end of that week, though, she had me doing it. It was better than wearing a ski mask.

I flicked on my flashlight and directed it at the ground. In the fall, Mr. Huffman hadn't been sure he was going to sell us the farm, so he'd plowed the ground. Ridges and furrows littered with the remains of corn stalks created a path I had to tread carefully if I didn't want to twist an ankle out here alone.

This was the only time I regretted not having a house phone. Without my phone, I couldn't call anyone to tell them where I was headed. I'd swung by Russ' house in the hope that he'd come with me, but he wasn't home. With Stacey gone to Florida with her parents and baby Noah, no one else lived on Sugarwood grounds for me to tell.

I would have to be careful not to trip. Even if I did, I could still crawl back to the warmth and safety of my car. It wouldn't be fun, but I could make it before frostbite or hypothermia set in.

You're being silly, Nikki, I mentally lectured myself. *You're perfectly capable of walking through a field by yourself without a babysitter.*

I wove through our newly planted saplings, being sure to avoid the giant holes waiting for the remaining trees. The holes weren't extremely deep, but they were big enough for me to fit inside. If I tripped into one, I could definitely break an ankle or a wrist.

A light flashed up ahead, just inside the tree line.

My fingers switched off my flashlight before I could even think about it. The other light continued to bob between the trees. Whoever it was either hadn't seen me—they would have switched off their light if they had—or they weren't worried about someone else seeing them.

I was out here for a legitimate reason. It was my land, and I'd forgotten my phone. No one else should be out here. The chances that someone else had also forgotten their phone seemed slim.

Which left me with two options. I could head back to the safety of my car, drive over to Elise and Erik's house, and convince one of them to come back with me. Or I could sneak forward, grab my phone, and then hustle back to the safety of my car to call the police.

The first option was safer, but it almost ensured that whoever was out here would be gone before we could figure out who they were. Too much had happened concerning this farm for me to believe that this was some random person. For all I knew, it could be the other buyer, intending to sabotage our newly planted trees in the hopes that we'd give up and sell the land at a loss. I couldn't come up with a reason why they didn't go buy a piece of land somewhere else, but they obviously had one. Someone didn't want us to have this land. At least not peacefully.

The downed tree where I remembered setting my phone was only ten to fifteen feet away. All the holes between me and it had already been filled. I could creep forward without light. I'd put on my Uncle Stan's big jacket because it was the warmest thing I had. It was dark gray. The only pieces that could possibly stand out were my white mittens and scarf.

I sucked my hands back into the sleeves of my jacket. One less bright color to show up.

Get the phone. Get back to my car. Call the police.

I kept repeating that mantra over and over to myself as I crept forward one tree at a time, moving as slowly as I could so that my movement didn't draw the other person's attention.

I reached the tree and sank down into the dead grass beside it. I slid my hand along the trunk. My hand bumped something thin. It slid off the other side.

Crap.

This was still salvageable. I knew where it'd gone. All I had to do was carefully reach my arm over and hope I could get my hand around it.

I leaned forward. The light bobbed closer, and I froze, one arm dangling over the side of the tree, my white mitten sticking out. If I stayed as still as a spooked deer, maybe they'd think the mitten was abandoned, dangling from a tree branch.

The figure was too small and much too thin to be a man. The edge came off my tension. I'd taken self-defense classes. I could probably get away from a woman if she noticed me. Assuming she didn't have a gun, of course.

The angle of the beam shifted, throwing light momentarily across the face of the other person.

Ashley Jenkins.

18

*M*y arms felt numb, like my brain and body weren't connected anymore.

Elise hadn't found a link between Ashley and the other buyers for this farm because there wasn't one. She hadn't been trying to stop the sale so that someone else could buy the property. She'd been trying to stop—or at the very least delay—the sale until she could find whatever it was she was out here looking for.

I struggled to keep my breathing steady and low and inched my arm further forward toward my phone. I had to get my phone and call the police.

There was only one thing that would be worth going to all this risk and trouble for. Ashley must have been the one who killed Lee Mills, and something out here could connect her to the crime. It hadn't been a problem when the field was farmland. Mr. Huffman rode through the field in a tractor or a combine.

Once Russ and I bought it, though, we'd have a half a dozen people walking all over out here to dig holes and plant trees.

She must not realize that whatever was out here couldn't be used as evidence. Tom McClanahan wasn't a criminal lawyer. She wouldn't have any reason to know the laws on evidence and chain of custody. Or maybe she did, but she also knew that whatever was out here was so condemning that, if the police ever got it, it wouldn't matter that they couldn't use it directly. They'd know she'd done it, and they'd keep investigating her until they found something else that could prove her guilt.

If I could get my phone and get someone out here before she left, we might still be able to find what was out here. Case and Daphne would both be cleared.

My fingers came up short of the ground. I'd have to move my torso further over the tree to get my phone.

Ashley turned her back to me, her flashlight aimed at the base of the trees in front of her. She moved the dead leaves out of the way with what looked like a rake or one of the shovels that we'd left behind from the trees—I couldn't see for sure in the dim light.

I leaned forward. The log moaned, and a branch snapped. I'd put too much of my weight on it.

I ducked down behind it, phoneless. Crap. Big steamy pile of crap.

Maybe she would think it was the wind or natural forest sounds.

Her flashlight switched off. Not the action of someone who thought the wind did it.

Now I had to decide whether to hunch here and hope she

didn't spot me or to crawl away until I put enough distance between us to make a break for my car. Running was out of the question. The ground was too uneven. I'd trip for sure. So did I think I could speed walk faster than she could?

And if she recognized me, I didn't have enough against her for the police to arrest her. She'd be out there and I'd be out there. If she'd killed Lee, she might very well start planning a way to kill me as well.

I couldn't let her see me.

I waited, trying to both count to keep track of the time that had passed and pray all at once.

Thirty seconds passed.

The sound of leaves rustling and crunching reached my ears. It was soft, like Ashley was trying to move away quietly.

The wind kicked up, and the trees around me groaned, their branches knocking together. It wiped out the sounds of the rest of Ashley's retreat.

I had to be sure she was far enough away, grab my phone, and walk-run to my car. I might be too late now to have someone catch her out here, but at least she wouldn't know I'd spotted her.

I counted another twenty seconds and then pulled myself up into a crouch. I peeked over the fallen tree. The wind made it impossible for me to hear anything, so I scanned the trees for movement or a shape that looked out of place.

Nothing.

She must have headed back to wherever she'd parked her car. It hadn't been on the road where I'd left mine. Once she reached her car, she might try to drive around the field and see if she could spot the vehicle of whoever was out here with her. Even if she didn't recognize my car right away, she'd be able to write down my license plate and eventually put the pieces together.

I had to get out of here before she got to her car.

I laid belly-first on the tree and reached for where my phone had fallen. I was fairly certain she wouldn't be back tonight and that she hadn't yet found what she was hunting for. If I could get Erik and Elise back here, we might be able to find whatever it was first. Now that Ashley was gone, I'd call them on the way to my car.

My fingers brushed something too smooth to be naturally occurring. Got ya.

Fiery pain exploded in the back of my head, and everything went dark.

19

*T*he air smelled musty, like old vegetation. And heavy.
No, that wasn't right. Heavy wasn't a smell. My
brain felt tangled up and knotted, like a five-year-old's shoelace.
The pain in my head was worse than the most severe migraine. I
felt as if I were blinking my eyes, but nothing changed from
opened to closed.

The last thing I remembered I was out in the woods, trying
to find my phone, so I could call Erik and Elise for something.
What did I want them to look for? It'd been important.

I closed my eyes—or at least thought I did—and drew two
slow breaths. First things first. I'd been in the woods, and it'd
been windy, so a branch must have fallen from a tree and hit me.

That could be why I felt so heavy. Maybe it'd paralyzed me.
Dear Lord, let me not be paralyzed. If I was, there were worse
things, though. I was alive. Alive and paralyzed was much better
than dead. People lived full, wonderful lives in wheelchairs all
the time. They even competed in the Paralympics.

Focus.

I wriggled my fingers. Those still worked. I tried to move my toes. Nothing. No, wait. My toes were moving in my boots. I could feel them hitting the top. My feet just didn't have room to move. They must be pressed up against the tree I'd been leaning over.

The tree I couldn't see.

So I wasn't paralyzed, but I was likely blind. Could you be blind and a lawyer? A lot of what I did required reading facial expressions.

I dragged my mind back. Now wasn't the time for that. Previous experience had taught me that, if I was lying out in the woods in the winter, I didn't have long before hypothermia set in. I was warmer than I'd expected, probably because of my coat, but I couldn't stay out here forever.

If I was blind, I had to figure out exactly what direction I was facing. Once I did that, I could search the correct side of the tree, find my phone, and tell it to call 911. Thanks to ending up in an upside-down car in a ditch before my wedding, I now knew exactly what capabilities my phone had.

Actually, I might not even need to find it. If it were near enough, I could simply tell it to call 911.

"Hey, Siri."

My voice sounded too close to my head. On top of me somehow, like it had nowhere to go.

My phone didn't answer.

Don't panic, Nik, I told myself. *You can pray, but you can't panic. Panicking won't help.*

I sent up a quick prayer. Maybe my scarf was muffling my words. I wriggled it down off my mouth and tried again.

Nothing.

I'd have to find it. I stretched my hand in the direction that the tree had to be based on my wedged feet. My fingers hit a barrier. It was cold and left something on my fingers that reminded me of writing with chalk. My mitten must have gotten caught on a twig as I fell and came off. This hand was colder than the other one.

I touched the solid object again. Not a tree. It felt more like frozen dirt. Unless the blow to my head had destroyed my equilibrium, I couldn't be lying on my side in such a way that it would both block my feet and feel like a wall.

I tried to stretch my arms and legs out, but something blocked me on every side.

Dear God, no. No no no. I had to be in the fetal position down in one of the holes we'd dug for the trees. It was the only thing that made sense.

I moved my hand upward a few inches. My fingers connected with rough material like the burlap that we'd wrapped the trees' root balls in to transport them.

That explained why my lower body felt heavy, but I could still breathe. I was in one of the tree holes, and whoever threw me down here covered me in a piece of burlap before burying me alive. We'd had that one warm day where the snow melted a bit. The burlap we'd cut off the dead trees must have gotten wet and then froze solid again when the temperature dropped. It created a roof for me.

If I couldn't find a way out, it'd create a coffin.

A flash of memory. Ashley Jenkins' face in the glow of a flashlight.

That's what had been so important for me to call Erik and Elise about. I'd come out to the bush because I'd forgotten my phone, spotted Ashley, and figured it out.

She must have sneaked around behind me, intending to check if she'd been seen. When she saw me, she bashed my head with the shovel. I hadn't heard her because of the wind in the trees—wind I couldn't hear now. I should have realized right away that it was too quiet.

Maybe she didn't even realize I was still alive when she threw me in here. She might have simply wanted to get rid of my body in the easiest possible method. She couldn't exactly dig a better hole for me. The ground was frozen solid now.

That frozen ground and the burlap she'd tossed over me would also prevent me from clawing my way out. I pushed on the burlap, but it didn't budge. I wasn't deep, but I was deep enough that I couldn't shove the dirt off of me, either.

Ashley had effectively buried me alive.

20

*T*he hole felt like it shrunk down until it would crush me. My heart beat at twice its normal rate, and my breathing doubled. If I didn't die from hypothermia first, my air pocket would soon run out, and I'd suffocate.

I couldn't let that happen. I had to hang on as long as possible. I didn't know how long I'd been unconscious, but it'd been after dark already when I left home. Mark would be worried soon. He'd likely call Russ or Elise to check in on me. They'd find I was missing, and eventually someone would spot my car.

All I had to do was conserve my air until that happened.

The freaked-out I'm-too-young-to-die-like-this feeling in my chest was making me breathe too fast. I used to watch the show *The Mentalist,* and Patrick Jane once kept someone from bleeding out after a gunshot wound by getting them to slow their breathing down. The only problem was, I couldn't remember how he did it. Something about getting them to focus on his voice. He'd coached them.

My pulse kicked up another notch, pounding in my ears. My legs and back hurt so much from being tucked into a ball that they almost rivaled the pain in my head. How was I supposed to calm down? I didn't have a coach. Women in labor got coaches. I was here alone, in a hole, with no way out. I didn't have anyone to talk to me or to talk with.

That wasn't entirely true. If I believed what I said I believed, then God knew I was in this hole. Prayer had helped me calm down my anxiety attacks, and I knew that prayer had the same effects on the ability to cope with stressful situations as meditation did. I'd even read a study done by Bowling Green State University that showed that spiritual meditation or prayer could reduce the number of migraines their test subjects experienced.

I'd pray. I'd pray until someone either found me or I was reunited with my Uncle Stan.

I focused my mind on praying to get out of this hole, but also on Mark and on Stacey and on Russ and Elise and Erik and Mandy and everyone else I cared about. My breathing slowed, and I kept on praying.

My feet went numb, and my hands tingled. My body wanted to shiver, but each time a shiver hit, pain arched through me.

I was praying again for Mandy when a sound that reminded me of her voice came from above. Her voice and Russ' voice. I couldn't hear words. I wasn't even sure I heard sounds. It was more that I felt like I heard the cadence of their speech. Mandy's fast verbal diarrhea of words followed by the pause and slower staccato of a response that Russ would have made. It might all be in my head, the oxygen depleting around me and causing hallucinations. I couldn't get enough into my lungs anymore. It wouldn't be long now.

I let my eyes drift shut. There wasn't anything to see anyway.

Scraping noises.

My eyes popped open. I hadn't imagined that.

I couldn't think of anything to say so I screamed, as loud and as long as my dry throat would let me. If there was someone up there, I needed to make them hear me, even if it burned up all my remaining air. If they didn't hear me, I wouldn't last long enough for someone else to find me.

The answering yelp from above me definitely sounded like Mandy. The scraping noises sped up.

My lungs started to burn like I was trying to hold my breath underwater for too long.

How long could a brain survive without oxygen? It was six minutes, wasn't it? That was how long you had to start CPR.

I could make it six minutes. If whoever was up there kept digging, they'd reach me in time. Even if I'd passed out, they could do CPR.

The sounds grew closer, and my lower body felt lighter somehow. The burlap tore back, and dirt showered down over me.

I gasped in a full breath, so cold I almost choked on it. Then another. It tasted so good.

Two hands grabbed my right arm and brought me to a sitting position. My legs didn't want to work. Pins of pain shot through them, like they'd been asleep too long.

Another set of hands grabbed my other arm, and then I was out of the hole. Warm arms wrapped around me, a dirty hand—

like they hadn't had a second shovel so they made do—pressing my cheek into a chest so soft it had to belong to a woman. And the smell of cinnamon and yeast dough.

I hadn't imagined Mandy's voice. No one else smelled like that.

"Ashley Jenkins," I tried to say, but my voice came out in a squeak.

"There's blood frozen in her hair," Mandy's voice said, a higher pitched sound than anyone her size should have been able to make. "I'm sure she's bleeding. You need to call an ambulance."

"I already called an ambulance." Russ's face swam into view. He held something up in front of my face that I could only assume was his phone. "They're on the line, and they're on their way."

"Tell them." My words were audible this time, but every one hurt. "Ashley Jenkins."

ime passed in a blur after that, with small pieces standing out.

Mandy and Russ arguing over which one of them would ride in the ambulance with me—Mandy won.

Passing through a crowd of familiar faces as they wheeled me from the ambulance into the hospital on a stretcher. Elise and Mark's mom hovering by the sides for as long as the staff would let them.

And then they must have put me out to clean and stitch my head wound. Or I passed out. The next thing I remembered was opening my eyes in what had to be a private room, based on its size, but it was anything but private.

Mandy sat in the chair next to my bed. My hand must have been in hers a long time because it felt moist and hot. I eased my head to the side to look at where our hands lay. Dirt still caked her cuticles and under her fingernails. I hadn't imagined that part, then. Mandy had actually gotten down on her hands and knees to dig the dirt off of the top of me.

Russ stood behind her, trying to touch as few things as possible, a little bottle of hand sanitizer clutched in one large fist. Mark's mom sat in another chair on my other side, and I could see the tops of Elise, Megan, and Grant's heads over the tips of my toes as they all sat on the floor, lined up along the wall.

Physically, I felt like I'd been run over by a lawn roller, but the smile inside of me was huge. It was official. I was a Cavanaugh. They'd all turned out for me even without Mark around. Presumably, Mr. Cavanaugh had all the kids, and Erik—I hoped—was finding Ashley Jenkins.

"You're awake." Mark's mom leaned forward and kissed my forehead. "You're going to be fine, and I've already called Mark and your parents. Mark's on his way home, but I told him not to speed, that we've got you until he gets here."

A warmth filled my chest. Any time in the past when I'd woken up in a hospital room, I'd had to ask if I was okay and where everyone was. Mark's mom made sure that—whatever else might be the case—I didn't need to worry about those things. I would attribute it to her mom training except that I'd woken up in a hospital room with my mom before and I still had to ask for details. Then again, my mom tended to think that she only had to mention things to me if they were a problem I needed to deal with personally. If everything was fine, she felt no need to talk about it.

Considering that Mandy and Russ dug me out of a shallow grave, they were all going to have a lot of questions for me. I wanted mine answered first. "How did you find me?"

Nothing else mattered quite as much as that one. Had they not found me when they did, I wouldn't have made it.

"Mark," Elise and Russ said at the same time.

A smattering of laughter trickled around the room.

Elise came to the end of my bed and rested her hands on the foot railing. Out of the corner of my eye, I thought I saw Russ cringe. He hated hospitals and germs so much that it spoke to how much he cared about me that he was still here.

"Mark got worried when he couldn't reach you," Elise said. "So he called me."

She would have tried calling and texting me as well. Wherever my phone was now, I'd have a list of messages to get through.

She ran a hand along the bed rail. "When you weren't at home, either, I called Russ to see if you were with him."

"Which of course you weren't," Mandy piped up, "because he was with me. We said we'd meet Elise to help look for you."

I glanced toward Mandy, making sure my head didn't move. Russ had been with Mandy. He hadn't told me that. I thought he was at a Rotary Club meeting.

Mandy squeezed my hand. "Mark remembered he'd helped you install the Phone Finder app on your new phone, so I logged into your account." There was pride in her voice, but almost a touch of shame as well.

Mark had my login information, but the way Mandy said it make me think she'd hacked my account. I wasn't going to ask. I wasn't sure I wanted to know. Whatever she'd done, I'd forgive her because I'd be dead if she hadn't.

Russ' chest puffed out, making him look a bit like a penguin, squatty but proud. "I recognized the spot it showed as Mr. Huffman's field." He narrowed his eyes at me. "Which I told them you shouldn't be out in alone after dark."

I tried to hide my smile. I should have known I'd get a lecture from Russ at some point. "I didn't know anyone else would be out there."

"Doesn't matter," he said with a grumble.

"Anyway," Elise said, "we headed that way, but your phone started moving away from the field. When we saw your car was still there, I said I'd follow your phone and Russ and Mandy decided to head out to the planting site just in case."

My lungs felt flattened in my chest. Ashley had taken my phone. If they'd all followed it instead...

I couldn't even go there.

Elise's hands tightened around the bed rail, as if she'd mentally gone there as well. "Mark called me again to say someone had texted him from your phone saying they made a mistake moving to Fair Haven and getting married and that they'd be gone by the time he came home. Don't try to find them."

Elise's phrasing made it clear neither of them believed I'd sent the text. Still, if there'd even been a moment that Ashley made Mark wonder if I loved him—my throat felt too thick to speak.

I had to force the words out. "How did he know it wasn't from me?"

Elise shrugged, and the look on her face said she thought Mark and I might be weirdos, even for Cavanaughs. "He said it didn't sound like you. Something about the syntax?"

I snorted and covered my mouth. Mark and I spent most of our early friendship texting. If anyone would know how I wrote, the cadence of my sentences and the words I did and didn't use, it would be him.

Elise was still shaking her head, but it was slower now, like it carried the weight of what might have happened if he had believed it. "I called Mandy and Russ and told them I thought someone stole your phone and that you had to still be out there somewhere. Your phone disappeared from the app shortly after that."

"We must have walked a quarter of the way back to Sugarwood through the bush looking for you," Russ said. "We had to check every one of Mandy's theories. What if they covered your body with leaves? What if they'd tied you up in a tree?"

Mandy wrapped her second hand around mine. "What if they buried you alive?" Her voice caught.

I added my second hand to the hand pile we now had. I never would have expected one of Mandy's crazy theories to be the thing that saved me.

"I told her the ground was too hard for anyone to bury you alive." Russ ran his hands over his face and up into his hair. It stood on end, and he didn't bother to smooth it down. "She said we'd dug holes for the trees. Someone could have put you in one that was already dug. She wouldn't leave until I counted the holes and the remaining trees because the numbers should match."

They didn't. They'd found one more tree than hole.

So many things could have gone wrong to keep them from finding me.

Heat burned in a little ball at the base of my neck. It hadn't been enough for Ashley to interfere with our land purchase to buy herself time to find whatever she'd lost out there all those years ago. It hadn't been enough for her to try to kill me even though I didn't have any solid evidence against her and she couldn't even be sure I'd seen her face. She'd then taken my phone and sent Mark that message.

From the perspective of a killer trying to cover their tracks, it was a smart move. If everyone thought I'd taken off of my own free will, they would be less likely to look for me. I wouldn't be a missing person if I told them I was leaving.

But I wasn't sure that was the only perspective Ashley was working from. If I'd gone missing, Mark would have kept hoping and hunting for me for years, maybe for the rest of his life. By making it look like I'd left him, Ashley had to be hoping she'd still have a chance with him.

It was sick and twisted in a way that made me simultaneously want to hit something and throw up.

"Did they find Ashley?"

Elise dropped her gaze to the end of the bed. "They did. She didn't have your phone."

"I can give my testimony to Chief McTavish and have her arrested for attempted murder."

For a full two breaths, Elise continued to stare at the bedding. She finally lifted her gaze to mine.

Right. I got it. We couldn't have her arrested for anything. Chief McTavish could bring her in for questioning based on my testimony that she'd been in the area. But I hadn't seen who hit me or threw me in the hole and buried me alive. It was possible someone else did it. A good defense attorney like either of my parents would argue that proximity to a crime doesn't make someone a criminal. Ashley could have been out in the woods for any number of reasons, and I saw her leave before I was hit.

We had one chance. "Ashley was looking for something in the woods. I went out there because I forgot my phone"—I directed a see-I-had-a-good-reason-for-being-there look at Russ —"and saw her searching. I think she delayed the sale of the farm because she wanted to find it before one of our workers stumbled on it. I suspect whatever it is will connect her to Lee Mills' murder."

Elise's hand was already moving for her cell phone. "I'll call Erik. The chief should be able to hold Ashley at least while they search."

ark and my doctor were discussing the results of my latest CT scan the next day when Chief McTavish knocked on the doorframe.

"My apologies for interrupting," he said, and he sounded like he meant it.

My doctor slid the scans back into the envelope. "I'll start the paperwork for getting you out of here, but I want you back in a week for a follow-up scan."

Mark shook his hand again. "I'll make sure she gets here."

My scans had shown a microscopic bleed, but it hadn't grown any larger, suggesting it'd sealed itself. Unfortunately, I was banned from driving until the doctor could be sure my brain was absorbing the blood—a sign that everything was well and healing.

Mark motioned McTavish to the chair next to my bed. "I'll go sign for your release so we can get you home."

I thought about blowing him a kiss, but in some ways, Chief

McTavish was his boss. I could hear my mom's voice lecturing in my head about professionalism even as the thought of blowing kisses formed.

Chief McTavish sank into the chair next to me, his back stiff. He held out a pale green envelope, the size of a card. "From my wife."

I slid it open. It was a beautiful card signed with only their first names. No message. But I saw it for what it was. In the few exchanges I'd had with Mrs. McTavish, she'd seemed lonely. Now that Chief McTavish was staying on permanently as Fair Haven's chief of police, this must be her way of reaching out. As the wife of the county medical examiner, I probably seemed like her safest bet for where to start making friends.

I'd make sure to give her a call once I was back home. And once I got my phone back. Presumably Ashley had tossed it.

"Thank you," I said.

Chief McTavish nodded like he wasn't entirely comfortable with changing our roles, but he loved his wife, so he likely didn't have much of a choice.

He rested his hands on his knees in a casual-professional posture. "We found what Ashley Jenkins was looking for."

He pulled out a photo and handed it to me.

The image was a close-up of one of those gold name neck-laces. The cursive script spelled out *Ashley*. Rusty flecks covered it.

I handed the picture back. "Is that blood?"

It seemed almost impossible that there would still be blood evidence on it after so many years and exposure to the elements. Rain and snow alone should have taken care of any DNA.

One side of McTavish's mouth lifted. "No, but she didn't know that."

Nice. Ashley had proved that she was scared of that necklace. She wouldn't have gone to so much trouble otherwise. It wasn't a stretch that she could be convinced it still had Lee Mills' blood on it and that the police could get a DNA match from it.

I shifted myself up further in bed. I was already dressed and ready to go, but Mark had insisted I rest until I was officially able to leave. Now having to sit here felt restrictive. My body wanted to move.

"Did she confess?"

The half smile slipped from McTavish's face. "Not entirely. Apparently, Mr. Mills stole a rather large sum of money from her car when he broke into it. Ashley didn't report it missing because she didn't realize it at first, and"—he glanced back over his shoulder in a way that made me think he was sharing more than he technically should have been—"she acquired it through means that weren't entirely legal."

Oh my. That could mean drugs, but my instincts said it was more like prostitution. I didn't know what she'd looked like before she had all her plastic surgery, but she must have been truly desperate to go to those lengths to get it.

"She went to Lee Mills' regular spots that night, looking for him," McTavish continued. "She found him alone in the field, drunk and surly. Their argument turned physical, according to her. He knocked her down, and she grabbed the closest thing to defend herself—an empty beer bottle."

I gingerly touched my fingers to the stitches in my scalp. I'd always have a scar there. "I'd be more likely to believe her story of self-defense if she hadn't hit me in the head and tried to bury my body."

The expression on McTavish's face actually looked sad, and my stomach clenched.

"She's not claiming self-defense. She's claiming he was alive when she left him. After she hit him, he grabbed for her neck. He missed and got her necklace, tearing it off. She was scared enough that she ran away."

A jury wasn't likely to believe her any more than I did. "And what's her excuse for me?"

"She admits to being out in the bush, but she says she heard a sound and didn't stick around to see what it was."

In other words, she claimed she wasn't the one who hit me and threw me in a hole. "What about my phone and the text she sent to Mark? That connects her directly to what happened."

Chief McTavish's pointy chin and red hair normally reminded me of a fox. The droop in his expression now made him look more like a basset hound. "We got a warrant for her car and apartment, but your phone wasn't there."

"What about the shovel or whatever she hit me with?" There was a frantic note to my voice that I didn't like but couldn't seem to control.

"It was a shovel. We found it nearby. We couldn't get any useable prints off of it." He glanced at my shoulder as if he were considering patting it. "I'm sorry. For now, we're letting her go."

23

*M*ark maneuvered out of his parking space in the hospital parking lot. "What does that mean for Case?"

I'd never been so glad that Mark was driving. After my conversation with Chief McTavish, my head was hurting for a reason other than the blow to the back of my skull. The police were going to investigate Ashley, but unless they found something, she might get away with killing Lee Mills and attempting to kill me.

One good thing had come out of it all. "Chief McTavish is asking the district attorney to drop the charges against him. He no longer believes Case is the most likely suspect, and Ashley created more than enough reasonable doubt for a jury. And they won't be pursuing charges against Daphne, either. Ashley saw Lee alive after Daphne left him."

Mark barely brought the car up to speed limit. With the doctor's warning that I needed to be extra-careful about any further head trauma until I healed, he'd probably be driving me around like he was an eighty-year-old man for the next week.

"We know that Ashley saw him after Daphne left because Ashley described him as drunk," he said, never taking his eyes off the road.

I nodded. Hopefully he'd catch the movement in his peripheral vision. "That, and McTavish said they found a witness who saw Daphne walking back to town around the same time that Ashley said she was confronting Lee."

Mark smiled, complete with dimples. "Then I think that means your favor to Grady Scherwin is officially paid."

Paid with interest, if he asked me.

Elise had promised me that she and Erik would walk the route Ashley probably took from the field to her apartment and see if they could find my phone. It was a long shot, and an even longer shot that she wouldn't have wiped her fingerprints off after texting Mark, but it was all we had.

We grabbed a burner phone for me on the way home. I hadn't given up hope on getting my real phone back, and to replace it, we'd have had to leave Fair Haven anyway. Mark wasn't keen on me going very far from the hospital where the doctor knew my condition. I figured I had to give him that one. After all, I had almost died. Again.

I texted all the people who'd need my number in the interim. If I hadn't been sure that I now had a whole tribe of people who cared about me, I would have been sure after I finished sending out my number. My fingers were tired.

I'd just sent the final text when Russ called.

"I wasn't sure if I should say anything," he said after grilling me about how I felt. "Wayne Huffman called."

There couldn't possibly be more trouble, especially now that Ashley knew we were on to her. She wouldn't be tampering with anything in the near future.

Besides, the money had cleared, and most of our trees were in.

We'd pulled up next to our house. I motioned for Mark to wait. I didn't want to risk moving and having the call drop. I wasn't sure how sensitive this phone would be about cellular dead zones.

"Everything okay?" I asked Russ.

My voice actually sounded fairly calm. Maybe my brain realized that, compared to being buried alive, any problems with the property were small and manageable.

Russ laughed his Santa Claus laugh, and I could imagine his body shaking. "Not this time. He wants to take us all out to dinner to celebrate the sale."

I put Russ on speaker so that Mark could hear, and we picked one of the days Mr. Huffman had suggested. Since Mark wasn't even going to allow me to walk the dogs on my own until after my next scan, I might as well take every opportunity I could to get out of the house.

~

WE'D SETTLED ON A SALT & BATTERY FOR OUR CELEBRATION dinner. Mark and I rarely ate in the restaurant itself, so it was a nice change. The interior smelled amazing—like fried food and tartar sauce. The tables reminded me of polished driftwood, with enough dings and crags to give them character. In the middle of our table, they'd placed a basket of popcorn.

Mark pulled my chair out for me as if I might break. If he was this careful with me now, I could only imagine what would happen if I were ever really injured.

Actually, that wasn't a bad thing. It was a good one. I'd never have to wonder if he'd take care of me if I couldn't take care of myself. I knew he would. Not everyone had that kind of security in this world. Daphne's past was a perfect example. Mark had even sat up with me last night when I'd had a nightmare and couldn't sleep.

Mrs. Huffman gave me a grandmotherly smile. "Such a gentleman."

I lifted a hand toward my head but stopped short of touching the injury. I'd ended up having to put my hair up in a ponytail to hide the stitches. "He's babying me a bit right now."

I filled her in on what had happened, leaving out the details and only explaining it in broad strokes. I'd gone out into the bush and was hit in the head by a woman involved in the case I'd been investigating to build a defense for a client.

The color faded from around her lips, leaving a stark white line that made her pink lipstick look the shade of cotton candy. Mr. Huffman laid a hand on her arm.

"I didn't mention it," Russ said.

He spoke the words almost under his breath, as if he couldn't believe I'd bring up something like that at a celebration meal. Or at all. If Russ had his way, he'd pretend nothing bad ever happened.

Hadn't Mr. Huffman said she liked to watch crime shows? I was sure he had. Though watching a TV show you knew was make-believe and hearing about a true crime did tend to affect people differently. I shouldn't have dropped it on her like that, assuming she'd be okay hearing it.

The waiter came and took our order. I got onion rings on the side even though my order already came with French fries. Today I was going to eat whatever I wanted to celebrate the fact that I was still alive to eat. That, and I'd woken up this morning hungry enough to actually make pancakes for breakfast rather than grabbing an apple or a yogurt from the fridge. My body must be thinking that if I was going to be attacked, it needed to store up extra energy reserves.

The Huffmans shared their plans. They were going to visit their son first in Grand Rapids. They wanted to look at some of the inclusive retirement villages there that provided weekly housekeeping to their tenants. They'd put their house on the market. The farm wasn't the only thing they'd been struggling with lately. Even the upkeep of their home had become too much. Once they had a lease signed for a place to live, they were going to take their first-ever overseas vacation.

"The honeymoon I always promised her," Mr. Huffman said.

Mrs. Huffman smiled at him, but it looked skin-deep to me. "It's the right decision, but I'll miss that house."

I could see grieving when the time came for Mark and me to finally leave our home. My eyes actually burned at the thought.

Thank you, head wound. The last time I'd had a head injury, it'd made my moods swing. It seemed like this one was going to make me weepy.

The pressure in my head from trying not to cry made the blood pulse in my wound. I fished around in my purse for the extra-strength ibuprofen my doctor prescribed. I pulled one out. It should be fine to take since it'd been six hours since my last dose, and I had a full stomach. The first one I took made me queasy, but Mark had said it was because I should be taking them with food.

Mark watched my every move. "You feeling okay?"

I nodded. I couldn't seem to get the words out around that irrational lump in my throat.

"Did they arrest the woman who hit you with the shovel?" Mr. Huffman asked.

The pill slipped from my hand and rolled under the table. The urge to cry vanished and left a cold numbness in its place.

When I'd told them the story, I hadn't said I was hit with a shovel.

24

*N*ot only had I not said I was hit with a shovel, I hadn't said I was buried alive. There'd be no reason to assume the person who hit me used a shovel. I'd said I was out in the bush. The most obvious thing to assume was that I'd been hit with a tree branch. Even a baseball bat or a tire iron were more common bludgeoning tools than a shovel, statistically speaking.

When the topic first came up, Russ said he hadn't told them, so he didn't include the detail about the shovel, either. In fact, Russ might not even know. I'd been under the impression from my talk with Chief McTavish that it was one of those details the police planned to withhold to better help them identify the real assailant. The only people who knew about the shovel as far as I knew were me, Mark, and the police.

And the person who hit me.

Mr. Huffman and Russ were both staring at me. Mark's hand was on my knee. Had he caught it, too?

I needed to answer Mr. Huffman, but the words wouldn't form. My mind couldn't seem to register the obvious reason why Mr. Huffman would have known I was hit with a shovel. But the only reason he would have had to try to kill me was if he thought I was out there searching for evidence and that I might find something to point to him.

"Not yet," Mark said, breaking the awkward silence. "They haven't arrested her yet."

"I'm sorry. I dropped my medicine." My voice sounded more upset than was rational even considering the situation. "It's important. I need to find it." I turned to Mark. "Help me?"

I slid off my chair and bent my head under the table. My orange pill rested next to Russ' boot, in plain sight.

Mark knelt next to me and stuck his head under the table as well. Good thing it was a wide table or we'd have bumped into the Huffmans' knees.

Mark's gaze slid to the bright orange pill. He didn't reach for it. He knew I'd never take a pill I'd dropped on a public floor. He also knew that my pills weren't something truly important like antibiotics or blood thinners. Losing one didn't matter.

So the fact that he'd come down without question meant he'd also caught Mr. Huffman's slip.

It all made sense. Mr. Huffman had been struggling financially. Lee had taken his combine for a joyride. A combine was a million-dollar piece of equipment even ten years ago. The repairs would have made his insurance premiums go up and could have cost him his harvest. He knew kids were driving through his fields, destroying his crops. If he'd found Lee there, he might have lost his temper. He'd told me he'd started driving around at night, trying to patrol. He'd even said something about Royce Allen having a good reason for hitting Lee. That if more people had stood up to Lee the way Royce did, maybe it wouldn't have come to what it did.

The problem now was what we could do about it. We had no proof that he was even in the area the night of Lee Mills' death. Unless...it was a long shot, but he might have been the witness who saw Daphne walking away. I'd told the police he used to drive around. I directed them to him as a witness. He'd have had to tell them something or it could have seemed suspicious that, with all the activity on his property, he knew nothing.

Thanks to my head injury, I hadn't been able to keep my cool. Mr. Huffman clearly wasn't a stupid man. He might put the pieces together and take his wife out of the country on their "vacation" sooner than planned. It wouldn't look suspicious, and it would prevent the police from questioning him. They wouldn't have enough for an extradition if the Huffmans decided never to return.

We needed the police to take him in for questioning now.

But I had no way to call them that wouldn't look strange and tip Mr. Huffman off further.

"You two okay down there?" Russ asked. The tone of his voice said *This is getting awkward.*

I moved my finger over to Mark's hand and slowly wrote letters.

Call McT witness.

I slid out from under the table. Hopefully Mark would understand enough to know to ask Chief McTavish the name of the witness. If it was Mr. Huffman, Mark would have enough reasons to ask McTavish to bring him in.

"Did you find it?" Russ asked.

"It's gone."

Mark came up beside me. "We'll have to go to the pharmacy after, explain what happened, and see what the pharmacist suggests."

Russ and Mrs. Huffman nodded like that was the most reasonable thing in the world. Something about Mr. Huffman's delayed response made me think he knew my dive under the table was about something more than a lost pill.

Mark changed the subject to ask about whether they had any grandchildren. Partway through Mrs. Huffman's answer, he reached a hand down toward his pocket.

He gave an apologetic smile that even I almost believed. "I'm on call today. I have to take this."

His reason was brilliant. No one could even question it.

I was definitely a bad influence on him.

Mr. Huffman set his silverware across his plate. "We should be going anyway."

Mrs. Huffman gave him a startled look. Whether or not she knew about Lee Mills, she didn't know about me. She clearly had no idea why her husband wanted to leave so abruptly.

I had to stop them. "I was hoping we could hear the end of the story about your granddaughter. Mark shouldn't be long."

"I'm sure he won't be able to stay for that," Mr. Huffman said. "He must have a crime scene to get to or they wouldn't have called him."

He'd essentially called my bluff. Mark was either on the

phone for a legitimate work call—and therefore would need to leave immediately—or he was calling the police for some other reason that we were trying not to admit to.

Russ rose to his feet. "Well, thank you for the meal. Can't help thinking we should have paid after all the trouble we caused."

Mr. Huffman waved his hand and headed for the till rather than waiting for our waiter to return and ask if we'd like the check.

Russ moved around the table, as if to follow Mr. Huffman and argue more. My pill rolled out from under the table. Russ stopped next to it.

"Oh." Mrs. Huffman stooped and picked it up. She held it out to me. "Is this yours?"

I started shaking my head before she asked. Because if I admitted it was mine, they were going to want me to swallow it down, and the mere thought made bile pool in my throat. "Mine was pink. And tiny."

It was the best explanation I could come up with for why we couldn't easily locate it. The carpet was dark with colored speckles all over it. A tiny pink pill would blend right in.

The waiter handed Mr. Huffman his receipt. Mark was off the phone and heading for him. He didn't glance my way. I took it as a message to stall more.

I blasted Mrs. Huffman with a smile so big it probably looked crazed. "Actually, would you help me look around for a minute and see if we can find it? My doctor was firm that I needed to take all of them, and I'm not sure the pharmacist will be able to replace one single pill."

"I'll help too," Russ said.

His tone carried enough worry that I knew thoughts were flowing through his head about me contracting an incurable infection if we didn't find that pill. I would owe him an apology later.

They both got down on all fours.

Nice, Nicole. You convinced two people in their sixties to kneel down on the floor to help you search for a pill that doesn't exist.

Even though it was for a noble reason, I felt selfish. I went down on my hands and knees with them.

"Is something wrong?" the waiter's voice asked from above my head.

"She dropped an essential medication," Mark's voice this time. It was strangled as if he felt so guilty he could barely keep from blurting out the truth or he was trying not to laugh. Without seeing his face, I couldn't tell which. "We're all looking for it."

The next thing I knew both Mark and the waiter were searching the floor too. We wouldn't be able to eat in here again. In fact, based on how many people were staring at us, I wouldn't be able to show my face in town at all for a few weeks. It was a very good thing my parents lived over six hundred miles away.

On the upside, Mr. Huffman couldn't leave now. Not only was his wife invested in the search, but he'd look like a jerk. He might even feel like a jerk if there was any doubt in his mind about the pill. He'd seemed like a genuinely nice man—right up until he beaned me with a shovel, anyway.

Hysterical laughter bubbled up into me, and I turned it into a coughing fit to keep it contained. My head throbbed. I'd known emotional swings could come with a head injury—it wasn't my first one, after all—but I felt like a yo-yo.

A cold rush of air hit the back of my neck. I glanced over my shoulder. Erik stood in the doorway. Whether Mark called him directly or Chief McTavish had sent him didn't matter. The cavalry had arrived.

Erik stared at us, a *What the heck?* expression on his face.

I pinched my thumb and pointer finger together as if I'd trapped a miniscule pill between them and held up my hand. "Found it!"

25

*E*lise perched on her desk at the Fair Haven police station. She'd given her chair to me.

"At least you didn't pretend to drop a contact lens," she said. "The Huffmans might have bought it, but Russ would have given the game away."

Mark had picked up on some of my tactics, but Russ never would. Not only would he not want to, but he was a terrible liar. When we'd first met, and he'd been suspected of murdering my Uncle Stan, I could tell when he was hiding elements of the truth from me.

At least my ploy bought us enough time for Erik to reach us. Mark played a major role in that. He'd opened the conversation with Chief McTavish with, "The man who used to own the field where Lee Mills' body was found knew Nicole was hit with a shovel." McTavish dispatched Erik immediately.

Once the Huffmans were on their way to the station, Mark had filled me in on the rest of the conversation.

Chief McTavish had confirmed that Mr. Huffman was the witness who said he saw Daphne walking toward town that night. McTavish checked his witness statement. Mr. Huffman had described her as "that girl who was always with Lee Mills" and said that "he remembered her because he couldn't understand why a nice girl like her put up with him." That, coupled with his slip about the shovel, convinced McTavish that Mr. Huffman might have headed to his field after seeing Daphne, figuring that Lee was up to something destructive that she didn't want to be a part of.

The only reason he wouldn't have come forward with that information sooner was if he didn't want to be connected to the area at the time and give the police a reason to look at him. With his history with Lee, they would have. I'd accidentally forced his hand. He got away with it until today because the police were convinced that either Case Hammond, or more recently, Ashley Jenkins, killed Lee.

Mark rested a hand on my back. "We might as well go home. Someone will call us with an update if they get a confession from Huffman. And you know McTavish can't let you sit in on any part of these interviews. Not even with Mrs. Huffman. You're the victim."

It was scary sometimes how well he knew me. But wishing for a chance to be part of the questioning wasn't the only reason I wanted to stay.

After all I'd been through, it was hard not to always be afraid, and I didn't want to live my life that way. I couldn't keep doing what I loved if that happened. "If I stay here, it feels like I'm not just another victim. I don't want to go home and be the victim."

Mark leaned in and kissed my forehead. "Then we stay for as long as you need."

Elise pulled another chair over and went back to her paperwork. Mark left me with her to go grab some work of his own from his office at Cavanaugh Funeral Home. I settled in to read a book on my phone. Anderson called once with a question about a different case.

The second time my burner phone rang, I assumed it was him again.

"We need you to come down to the station to identify your phone," Chief McTavish said.

I swiveled around in the chair. I couldn't see him, so he must be calling from his office. "I'm still here."

"I should have known."

He ended the call and came through the door at the far end of the room. He had a clear evidence bag in his hand.

He stopped in front of Elise's desk. "Didn't your shift end an hour ago, Officer Scott?"

Elise held up her pen. "Paperwork." Her voice inflected up at the end, making it more of a question than a statement.

I hadn't realized she was sticking around for curiosity's sake and, probably, for my sake. I glanced at the papers in front of her. They were the same ones she'd been working on the last time I looked up. They'd been completed then.

McTavish pulled over a chair. "This place has gone to the dogs now that none of you are afraid of me anymore."

"I'm still afraid of you, sir," Elise said, but her lips pressed together as if she were trying not to smile.

McTavish sighed and placed the evidence bag in front of me.

The cell phone inside was the same brand, size, and model as mine, but it didn't have the blue sparkly cover I'd bought. Presumably, the person who took my phone would have tossed the cover to make it less recognizable.

The phone had clearly already been dusted.

"Did you find any useable prints?"

"No," he said. "Do you recognize this phone as yours?"

He hadn't said *only yours* when I asked about prints, but he might have been withholding that so that I could identify it as my phone without bias. "Not by sight, but it'll be easy to find out." I reached halfway toward the bag. "May I?"

McTavish nodded.

I opened the bag and took the phone out. I pressed my thumb to the Home key, but nothing happened. The screen should have at least lit up. Unless the battery was dead. Or whoever took it turned it off to disable the Phone Finder feature. It only worked when the phone was on, and Elise had said that my phone disappeared from the map suddenly.

I pressed the power button. The screen came to life, and I placed my thumb on the Home key again. The phone unlocked.

"It's definitely mine. Did Mr. Huffman have it?"

McTavish opened the evidence bag and held it out to me. "Unfortunately not. When you identified him as your suspected attacker, I sent out uniforms to search the path from where you were attacked to his home."

Calling him my *suspected attacker* grated on me, but McTavish had to remain neutral. Mr. Huffman hadn't confessed, and we'd been sure up until a few hours ago that Ashley was the one who killed Lee Mills and attacked me. Without Mr. Huffman's prints on my phone and without my phone in his possession, it'd be even more difficult to tie him to what happened to me.

"We think he tossed it out of his car because he realized that if he left it at the scene, it could lead people to you. Or your body."

A shiver ran down my arms. "And he had no reason to keep it."

Except that he had kept it for longer than it took him to throw it away. He'd taken the time to send Mark a text. He must have taken my phone because he wanted to know who else I might have told about any suspicions I had about him.

Obviously, he wouldn't have found anything. I hadn't suspected him at all. In the process of checking, though, he would have noticed all the texts and missed calls piling up from Mark. He must have decided he had to do something about it.

How had he accessed my phone in the first place? He didn't have my passcode. He didn't have professional hacking skills—if he had, they wouldn't have struggled for money the way they did.

My throat dried out, and my head felt fuzzy. When I'd woken up in that hole, I'd been missing my right glove. He must have pressed my thumb to the Home key. Once my phone was unlocked, all he would have needed to do to prevent it from locking again was keep it active. "He used my thumb to unlock my phone before he buried me."

Elise's pen clattered to the floor, revealing that she'd been listening rather than working the whole time. "You remember?"

"I don't. I figured it out." Something Chief McTavish said

about Ashley and the rusty spots on her necklace came back to me. "But Mr. Huffman doesn't know that."

26

_M_ark held my hand like he wasn't going to let go, like he could prevent me from going through with the plan Chief McTavish and I came up with. "If you do this, and he doesn't confess, you've put an even bigger target on yourself."

Chief McTavish moved further down the hallway, giving us some space.

I held Mark's hand up to my cheek. It was cold. It felt good against my overheated skin. "If he doesn't confess, he won't stick around Fair Haven just to hurt me. He'll take his wife and head out of the country, and he won't come back."

Mark shifted his grip to twine his fingers through mine. "You've always said you were a terrible liar. He might not believe you."

I was a terrible liar in my real life, when I was talking to a person I cared about. This wasn't my life. This was a case. This was a suspect. "Do you remember when we first met and you got so jealous because you thought I was flirting with Jason Wood? But I was only working him for information about my Uncle Stan's death."

Mark gave an I-know-I'm-walking-into-a-trap nod.

"I know how to work a suspect. It's one of the skills I come by naturally, thanks to my parents' DNA." It wasn't one I was always proud of. It wasn't a good quality to be able to read people and manipulate them. I'd just chosen to take what would otherwise be a character flaw and use it in the pursuit of good, sort of like how stubbornness and determination were the flip side of the same coin. "Please support me in this. Whether or not he felt he had a good reason to kill Lee Mills, he didn't have one to try to kill me. He made an assumption without proof. That's escalation. If we don't stop him now, he might someday hurt his wife if he thinks she'll turn on him."

I still believed that sweet lady knew nothing about Lee Mills' death or the attack on me. It'd be hard enough for her going forward if her husband went to prison. It'd be even worse if she had to live with him, not certain if he was guilty or not—or if he confessed to her that he was. My instincts told me it'd only be a matter of time before she couldn't take that.

I had to help stop this now before anyone else got hurt, by Mr. Huffman or by their own hand.

Mark leaned his forehead against mine. "I hated that feeling when you weren't answering your phone, and the truth ended up worse than I was imagining."

"I'm safe here." I tipped my head back and kissed him. "Chief McTavish will be with me the whole time."

He let go of me, his face stern but his lips going to the effort of giving me a smile. "Do your thing."

Chief McTavish walked me down the hallway. He didn't try to give me a pep talk or advice. Strangely, for the first time, I felt respected by him, not just tolerated. He was taking a risk on me. If Mr. Huffman didn't believe that I woke up long enough to see him, they'd have to let him go.

We were hoping he'd believe me and feel guilty enough to accept responsibility. If he believed me but didn't feel guilty enough, he could request a lawyer and this would all be over as well. A lawyer would quickly point out that if I'd really seen him, he wouldn't be getting a chance to confess. He'd already be arrested.

We were banking not only on my acting ability, but also on the average person's lack of knowledge about how the legal system worked. Ashley hadn't understood it well enough, and she worked for a lawyer. Hopefully the same could be said about Mr. Huffman.

Chief McTavish opened the door for me and pulled out a chair on the opposite side of the table from Mr. Huffman. He helped me into the chair, playing up my injury and accompanying fragility.

I sank into the chair and tried to look small. I pressed my knees together and folded one hand over the other in my lap. I'd heard it called the "fig leaf" position before because of the way it made the person look like they were hunching their shoulders and shielding the sensitive parts of their body. I personally thought of it as the "funeral" position. People tended to adopt it when they were in a situation that made them uneasy, like a funeral. It should say *I'm vulnerable. I'm trying to comfort myself.*

Mr. Huffman came from a generation that often still saw women as needing a male protector. My body language would send subconscious messages to him before it was my turn to say anything.

Chief McTavish took the chair next to me, staging the situation so that it would look like I needed him as a shield. "I asked Mrs. Cavanaugh here because, according to the Sixth Amendment, you have the right to confront your accuser."

That wasn't really how the Sixth Amendment worked. It actually allowed for cross-examination of witnesses in a criminal proceeding. McTavish's lie was close enough to test Mr. Huffman's knowledge.

"I already told you." Mr. Huffman laid his arms on the table in front of him like a blocker. "I didn't do anything to her or to Lee Mills all those years ago. If I had, she wouldn't have come out to lunch with my wife and me today."

McTavish made an *I'm listening* noise. "Do you know how head injuries work?"

I felt more than saw Mr. Huffman glance in my direction. I was trying to keep my gaze down.

"No," was all he said.

There was still too much iron in his voice.

"When someone gets hit in the head the way Mrs. Cavanaugh was," Chief McTavish said, "their brain experiences the equivalent of losing your Internet connection. It can cause temporary amnesia. Some of those memories will return as the brain heals."

Mr. Huffman's torso moved, probably in a shrug but I couldn't look up to be certain. "So?"

"So she remembered something about the night she was hit."

Chief McTavish let that hang in the air. He was waiting for Mr. Huffman to ask what, to show that he was at least a little unnerved.

Mr. Huffman sat in silence.

It wasn't a good sign for our dramatization. He suspected we were baiting him.

Chief McTavish angled toward me. "Mrs. Cavanaugh, I'd like you to tell him what you told me. Take your time."

McTavish emphasized my married name again. I wasn't Nicole here. I wasn't Nicole Fitzhenry-Dawes, attorney at law. I was a wife, triggering Mr. Huffman to think about his own wife and how he'd feel if someone did this to her. Hopefully.

"I was in and out. Most of the time I couldn't even manage to open my eyes. But I remember him"—I peeked up at Mr. Huffman—"I remember *you* taking my mitten off and pressing my thumb to my phone to unlock it."

I held my right hand up above the table enough for him to see it.

Mr. Huffman jerked slightly. It was a very specific detail. One we shouldn't have been able to guess.

Don't think too hard about it, I silently urged him. *Say something.*

The pause was stretching too long. In many cases, leaving dead air was a great way to trick people into talking. In this case, it could work the opposite way—giving Mr. Huffman time to talk himself out of saying anything more and into asking for a lawyer.

I couldn't look in Chief McTavish's direction. It'd all be over if I did.

But I had to do something. We were losing him.

I looked up and met Mr. Huffman's gaze directly for the first time since I entered the room. "I just want to know why you did it," I said softly.

I didn't have to fake the wobble in my voice. I didn't want to go home because I didn't want to think about how close I came to never going home again. I wanted to keep busy because, as soon as I stopped, I'd think about it. At night, when I was trying to sleep, I'd think about it. About how cold it'd been and how much I hurt. About how my lungs burned and I knew I was running out of air.

Mr. Huffman's eyes watered. McTavish shifted beside me.

Oh no. I'd said all of that out loud. I'd basically done the emotional version of streaking.

Mr. Huffman broke eye contact. "I thought you knew, and I was scared."

It was a partial confession. A partial confession wasn't enough. A good lawyer could brush it away in court. He hadn't actually said he'd killed Lee Mills.

I had to pull myself together and finish this.

I slid my hands across the table, closer to him. "Mr. Huffman, you always seemed like a good man to me. You sold me your field because of your good memories of my Uncle Stan. You're not a hardened killer. If you explain why you killed Lee Mills, the district attorney will give you a lighter sentence. They don't want to send good men to prison for the rest of their lives for one moment of poor judgment."

Two moments, but I wasn't going to push the point. If I could get him to confess to Lee Mills' murder, he'd be going to prison for enough time that whatever he got for my attempted murder wouldn't matter.

Mr. Huffman wiped his hands across his cheek bones. "I didn't plan to kill anyone. You have to know that. It wasn't what they call pre-planned."

I was pretty sure he meant premeditated. He must have lied about his wife watching crime shows. Most people would have been more interested in my work as a lawyer than in my trees. He'd been afraid to show interest, but also afraid that if he didn't show interest, I'd be suspicious.

"After Lee Mills nearly put us under with the damage he did to my combine and our crops," Mr. Huffman said, "I started driving by the field each night just to check on things. Every year, kids would drive into our field to do things they didn't want to be caught doing, but it didn't cause near the level of damage that Lee Mills did in that one night. Crop insurance doesn't cover that kind of damage."

The report I'd heard from Royce was that Lee stole Mr. Huffman's combine and took it for a joyride, damaging it. He hadn't also said Lee took that joyride through the unharvested field, running down the crops.

It was times like this that I wasn't entirely sure who the true bad guy was. Mr. Huffman shouldn't have done what he did, but Lee Mills was far from an innocent victim.

"You found him there that night?" I said softly to keep him talking. He still hadn't admitted to anything.

"I saw his girl walking back to town alone after dark. No reason I could think of for her to do that except he'd done something unforgiveable to her. I knew he'd still be out in my field. All I planned to do was hold him until the police came and charged him with trespassing and destruction of property. If I caught him red-handed, they couldn't overlook it like they had before when there was *no evidence* he was the one who did all that damage."

If the timing had been even slightly different for any of them —for Daphne, for Ashley, or for Mr. Huffman—they'd have seen each other with Lee.

Mr. Huffman pulled a handkerchief from his pocket, something rare anymore. He dabbed at his upper lip. "I heard yelling as I walked up. A male and a female voice. Whatever woman he was with sounded scared. I didn't see her face."

Ashley. So they had almost crossed paths. If she'd seen him, Mr. Huffman would have had a witness to him being there, and things might not have escalated. Or he would have killed Ashley as well. I hated to think it, but he had tried to kill me to cover his tracks.

"The woman was gone by the time I reached them. He had blood running down the side of his head, and he heaved something gold into the bushes."

Ashley's necklace.

"I don't honestly know what happened next. I remember thinking that if someone didn't stop him, he'd eventually hurt someone bad. The next thing I knew, I was standing over him and he wasn't breathing. I took off as fast as I could, and I didn't look back."

Whether I believed him or not that he didn't remember the actual murder didn't matter. He might have blacked out in rage, or he might have been saying that because he still couldn't bring himself to admit out loud what he'd done. Either way, we had our confession.

Just in time, too. I couldn't have continued this much longer. My head felt tired, my body felt oddly achy, and a knot of dread sat in my stomach that I was probably going to have to find a new lawyer after all. I wasn't sure I could stand facing Ashley every time I went into Tom McClanahan's office, knowing I'd almost gotten her arrested for a crime she didn't commit.

And if she ever found out, none of my paperwork would ever be properly processed again.

27

*M*y doctor stopped us before we were able to leave the hospital after my follow-up CT scan. "If you could stay a few minutes, I need to talk to you. Let me find us an empty room so we'll have some privacy."

Those were never words you wanted to hear from your doctor. Even with all the privacy protocols now in place, if my scans had come back good, he would have either called me later or told us in the hall.

"What happens if I have a brain bleed?" I whispered to Mark as we followed the doctor through the halls. "Will I need surgery?"

Just the thought of brain surgery made me dizzy. And, oddly enough, made me want my mom. I guess there were some situations where people were always going to be little kids wanting their mommy.

A janitor pushed a cart of cleaning supplies out of an exam room up ahead.

My doctor hurried over and held the door open for us. "This'll do."

His voice was much too cheery. Probably false cheery. Doctors were trained to hide their true emotions from patients. You couldn't break down and cry every time you had to tell someone they were dying, after all.

If I'd survived being buried alive only to die from the blow Mr. Huffman gave me to the back of the head, Anderson would soon be defending Russ for murder. Heck, I wasn't entirely sure Anderson wouldn't help him plan the murder so that Russ could get away with it and they wouldn't need to plan a defense.

Now my brain really was going to crazy town.

Mark slid his hand into mine. "You're going to be fine," he said. "I promise."

Easy for him to say. He wasn't the one potentially bleeding out into his cranium.

My doctor motioned to the two chairs in the room and leaned against the exam table himself. "Something came up in the course of your scans, and I wanted to make sure you were aware of it going forward."

I wanted to tell him to spit out whatever the news was rather than trying to cushion the blow, but my tongue had glued itself to the bottom of my mouth. Mark didn't say anything, either, probably assuming we'd find out what was going on faster if he didn't bludgeon my doctor with questions and let him talk instead.

"When the ambulance brought you in, you were in and out of consciousness, and we couldn't get much information from you. Your sister..." He glanced to the side like he was trying to remember her name.

There were only two people he might mean. Neither of them was my sister, but it'd be easy to mistake them for a sister. "Elise? Megan?"

"Elise." He smiled. "Elise tried to answer as many questions as she could."

I reached blindly for Mark's hand again. This was starting to sound like I had some pre-existing condition that they hadn't known about that would now cause complications.

"She didn't think you two were trying, and so she said she didn't think you were pregnant. But given you'd experienced a head trauma and might have needed surgery or strong antibiotics, we always have to be cautious. We drew some blood to test to be on the safe side."

They must have tested my blood for other things at the same time as they did the pregnancy test. Maybe they thought...actually, I couldn't think of anything else they would have needed to test my blood for. It wasn't like they could be concerned about my sugar levels or something. I hadn't passed out. I'd been hit in the head with a shovel.

Mark had a glazed-over look on his face like he'd been the one with the head injury.

Wait a minute. "I thought you said that something came up in the course of my scans."

"It did. When you went for your scan today, you told the diagnostician that you weren't pregnant."

It was a standard question. They asked it every time I had to have an x-ray or some other procedure where radiation was involved. The woman who did all my CT scans since the attack hadn't seemed to believe my answers, though, because she'd practically swathed me like a mummy in protective gear. "That's right."

"That's why I asked to speak with you. When your answers didn't match what she saw in your patient records, she pulled me aside. She thought you might not know."

Mark was grinning now, in a dopey I-think-you-just-said-I-won-a-million-dollars way.

The pieces finally slotted into place in my injured brain. And I wasn't sure whether to feel grateful that I wasn't dying or a tiny bit panicked. We did want a family someday, but Elise was right. We hadn't been trying yet. "You're telling me that I'm having a baby, not a brain bleed?"

My doctor looked like it took all his professional composure not to laugh. "Yes, that's exactly what I'm telling you. Congratulations, Mr. and Mrs. Cavanaugh. You're going to be parents."

LETTER FROM THE AUTHOR

One of the things that so many of you said to me after *End of the Line* was that you felt there were more stories left for Nicole, Mark, and the others to live. I hope you liked this latest installment in that journey, especially the surprise at the end. Nicole and Mark have always done things faster than normal, so it felt right that they'd also move quickly into this next stage of their lives together.

The next book, *Guilty or Knot*, will be coming out this summer. If you haven't yet signed up for my newsletter, please do. I announce new releases there first. I share recipes and other exclusives. And I give my newsletter subscribers a free ebook copy of *Sapped*, a Maple Syrup Mysteries prequel.

You can sign up at www.smarturl.it/emilyjames.

In the meantime, if you're looking for more to read, make sure you've picked up a copy of *Slay Bells Ringing*. Nicole and Mark's honeymoon is anything but average with a missing person and a mysterious illness.

Love,
Emily

ABOUT THE AUTHOR

Emily James grew up watching TV shows like *Matlock*, *Monk*, and *Murder She Wrote*. (It's pure coincidence that they all begin with an M.) It was no surprise to anyone when she turned into a mystery writer.

Alongside being a writer, she's also a wife, an animal lover, and a new artist. She likes coffee and painting and drinking coffee while painting. She also enjoys cooking. She tries not to do that while painting because, well, you shouldn't eat paint.

Emily and her husband share their home with a blue Great Dane, seven cats (all rescues), and a budgie (who is both the littlest and the loudest).

If you'd like to know as soon as Emily's next mystery releases, please join her newsletter list at www.smarturl.it/emilyjames.